Praise for

SHO[...]

Edward Stanford Childre[n...]
Young Quills Awar[d...]

'One of the best children's books I've read all year.'
The Literary Review

'Absolutely adored it!'
Emma Carroll, author of *Letters from the Lighthouse*

'A riveting adventure ... Eagle's writing grips the reader.'
Guardian

'Exciting, funny and full of warmth.'
LoveReading4Kids

'Full of suspense and mystery!'
Evie, aged 11, *National Geographic Kids*

'Absolutely sparkling, enchanting storytelling.'
Hilary McKay, author of *The Skylarks' War*

'A page-turning adventure.'
Nicola Penfold, author of *Where the World turns Wild*

'A brilliantly written and illustrated mystery ...
this is a gem of a book and is storytelling at its best.'
Kevin Cobane, *VIP Reading*

'A cracking read with superb storytelling.'
BookTrust

About the Author

Judith Eagle's career has included stints as a stylist, fashion editor and features writer. She now spends her mornings writing and her afternoons working in a secondary school library. Judith lives with her family and her cat Stockwell in South London. *The Stolen Songbird* is her fourth novel.

About the Illustrator

Kim Geyer studied textile design before taking up children's book illustration. She lives in London with lots of pets and kids – her biggest inspiration. Kim loves ice cream and sherbert Dip Dabs and being taken for walks by her dog, Dusty.

Also by Judith Eagle

The Secret Starling
The Pear Affair
The Accidental Stowaway

THE STOLEN SONGBIRD

Judith Eagle

ILLUSTRATED BY KIM GEYER

faber

First published in 2023
by Faber & Faber Limited
The Bindery,
51 Hatton Garden,
London, EC1N 8HN
faber.co.uk

Typeset in Garamond Premier by M Rules
Printed by CPI Group (UK) Ltd, Croydon CR0 4YY

All rights reserved
Text © Judith Eagle, 2023
Illustrations © Kim Geyer, 2023

The right of Judith Eagle and Kim Geyer to be identified as author
and illustrator of this work respectively has been asserted in accordance
with Section 77 of the Copyright, Designs and Patents Act 1988

*This book is sold subject to the condition that it shall not, by way of trade
or otherwise, be lent, resold, hired out or otherwise circulated without the
publisher's prior consent in any form of binding or cover other than that in
which it is published and without a similar condition including this condition
being imposed on the subsequent purchaser*

A CIP record for this book
is available from the British Library

ISBN 978-0-571-36314-8

Printed and bound in the UK on FSC® certified paper in line with our continuing
commitment to ethical business practices, sustainability and the environment.
For further information see faber.co.uk/environmental-policy

2 4 6 8 10 9 7 5 3 1

For Lucy and Margot

Prologue

1940

They left early, when it was still dark – before the lady who was meant to be looking after them woke up. They walked for miles and miles, through fields and woods, and along narrow twisting lanes banked by hedgerows. They didn't have a map, and the signposts that could've helped them were blacked out. It was common knowledge that the enemy must be thwarted at all costs.

As dawn broke, they shared the hunk of bread they'd stolen from the larder. They'd had to be quick – quick as lightning – the boy grabbing it when no one was looking, the girl hastily shoving it under her jumper. They worked as a team. They *were* a team, having grown up together since the girl had been orphaned, years and years earlier, and taken in by the boy's family.

Swallowing the last of the crumbs, they pressed on. To pass the time, they took it in turns to whistle – they were good at whistling – and they tried to outdo each other, showing off their prowess, with wilder and wilder and more complicated tunes.

At last, they came to a bus stop, and a bus that took them to Tonbridge, and then a train. Arriving at Charing Cross they turned out their pockets. Three conkers, two marbles and a boiled sweet. But no more money.

'We'll have to walk,' said the girl. Neither of them minded. They would've walked to the ends of the earth if they had to. They were going home.

It was dusk now, and the scents of London filled the air: soot, cabbage, chips and vinegar – smells that followed them up Saint Martin's Lane, along Tottenham Court Road, and up again to Camden Town. Other things were familiar too: the trams rattling by, the carts and the cars, the shops still open for business even though some of them were boarded up.

But it *wasn't* the same. For a start, there were people walking about in uniform and some of them were wearing tin hats.

'Wardens,' said the girl authoritatively. She was knowledgeable. Read the newspapers, knew everything. 'They help people find shelter when the bombs come.'

The air raids hadn't seemed real when they were in the countryside, but now they could see the evidence: great gaps where buildings had crumpled in on themselves; glimpses of streets where on one side there were mounds of rubble, and on the other side houses still standing, but with all the windows blown out. In a house on one corner, a hole gaped so big you could actually see straight inside. The wallpaper was a pretty rose print, pale pink blooms with green leaves, just like the girl had in her own bedroom.

She'd see it for herself soon.

By the time they had climbed the hill to Hampstead, their feet were dragging.

'Nearly there,' said the boy as they skirted past the houses that faced the heath.

It was still warm, right at the tail end of September,

and the front gardens were a mass of Michaelmas daisies and blowsy roses. The girl breathed deeply. She could already see the lamp by the gate. She remembered how its golden light glinted on the ivy and the laurel bushes. For the first time in ages, her chest relaxed.

They had just reached the drive when the wailing rose up. It started low and got higher and higher. It sounded eerie, like the shriek of a banshee, making the hairs on the back of the girl's neck prickle and stand on end.

'I think that means an air raid...' she said, her chest tightening again.

'We'll be quick,' said the boy firmly – now he was here, he couldn't wait any longer. 'Let's get him first and then we'll surprise her.'

The boy rushed along the side of the house towards the back garden. The girl could almost feel his joyful anticipation. She waited, listening out for the happy cries that would make the long arduous day worth it, but instead the sirens wailed again. She glanced up at the house, properly worried now. It was still dark.

'He's not here!' burst out the boy as he reappeared. 'She got rid of him!'

'She wouldn't do that, silly. Go back and check in the shed,' said the girl. 'Perhaps—'

High above came a droning sound. The girl looked up and for the first time felt a sharp blade of fear.

'Quick! We need to go in,' she shouted. They would go down to the cellar. They'd be safe there. She darted towards the house, trusting the boy to follow her. The droning was deafening now, like a swarm of bees.

She heard a rumbling noise, like faraway thunder, and then, much, much closer, a swish and a dull thwump followed by a shudder. A wall of air rushed at her, lifting her up and flinging her to the ground.

* * *

She lay quite still.

Everything was choked in black: billowing clouds of smoke in her eyes and her nose and her mouth, making her cough and splutter. A shower of dust and debris rained down. Fingers of fire leapt into the sky. Cinders floated in the air.

It was like being caught in a terrifying dream with dancing devils and hellish furnaces and ...

Except it wasn't a dream. It was real.

Much later, she got to her feet. The sky had turned a dirty, bruised yellow. Her ears were ringing.

Something very, very bad had happened.

'I can't see you, where are you?' the girl called to the boy.

But there was no answer.

Chapter One

1959

Nineteen years later

He was a large rabbit, at least the weight of five bags of sugar, but Caro Monday was strong.

Reaching into the hutch she hauled him out. It was a sizeable hutch, taking up a quarter of the cobbled yard, smelling of sweet hay and sawdust. The rabbit sighed happily and flumped against Caro as she wrapped her arms around him. His ears were soft as velvet, supremely comforting in the chill of the late afternoon air.

'I won't go, she can't make me,' she whispered into his warm fur. The rabbit, who was all white, apart from one ginger ear and a matching patch over his left eye, gave a little snuffle and she knew he was agreeing. 'You understand me,' she said. 'We'll wait here for Mum. She *will* come.'

But where *was* Mum? She was meant to have arrived home yesterday. Caro had been crossing the days off on the calendar, listening out for the familiar sound of her whistling 'The Flower Duet' as she walked up the street. It was the start of the school holidays and she had promised to help Caro build an outdoor gym. There was going to be a beam for balancing on, a pole to climb, and maybe even a trapeze. Once it was built, she would be able to start her training in earnest.

Caro was so looking forward to it she'd got out Jacinta's tools in readiness: the saw, the hammer, the pliers, and the nails in their screw-top jars. She had spent weeks scouring the Rubbles for the most useful odds and ends; she had collected all the scrap wood she could find. She and Horace had even marked out an area in the Rubbles where the gym was going to be constructed, and had cleared the ground, making sure it was tidy, level, and ready for building.

But building things was her mother's forte, and if

Jacinta didn't show up today, and Ronnie got her way, Caro couldn't see how she could build the gym on her own. And if she didn't have a gym, how could she practise? And if she couldn't practise, how was she ever going to make her mark?

Behind Caro, the door opened, and a chink of light illuminated the small yard. From inside the pub, the familiar sounds of clinking glasses and the hubbub of conversation drifted out, along with a whiff of tobacco, whisky and beer. The rabbit, who was named His Nibs and tended towards an air of refinement, sneezed.

'Caro,' said Veronica Rudd as she stepped outside, 'we've been through this a thousand times. My sister is poorly, she needs my help. And I need yours.'

Put like that it sounded so simple. But Caro knew it was far from simple. Veronica's sister lived miles away, 'up north'. 'Needing help' meant leaving the pub and leaving Caro.

And the problem was, Caro couldn't be left on her own.

Veronica Rudd was a fierce-looking woman – you had to be to run a pub, even if it was a tiny one tucked into a cramped space, under the arches, just along from the station at Waterloo. She rubbed her hands on her flowered pinny and sighed. As usual she was run off her feet: whizzing between the bar and the back kitchen, peeling potatoes for Caro's tea, totting up the monthly accounts, keeping the customers happy and pulling pints. But besides being fierce, Veronica Rudd was also fair; she loved Caro as if she was her own child. And Caro loved her back – for her fierceness, for her capability, for always being there. But Caro was stubborn, and Ronnie was stubborn too. 'A pint of bitter, Mrs Rudd, if you please,' called a customer from the saloon.

In answer, the publican kicked the door shut. If they wanted a drink, they'd have to wait. And wait they would; nobody dared quarrel with Ronnie Rudd. The real name of the establishment was The Railway Tavern. But everyone stuck to calling it Mrs Rudd's Pub.

'I'm not going to Great Aunt Mary's, Ronnie!' Caro burst out. His Nibs agreed with a sort of short, shocked quiver. 'I'd rather be sent away to boarding school!' At least there might be a gym there. 'If Mum knew what you were planning, she'd have a fit.'

'Boarding school!' Ronnie Rudd shuddered. 'Jacinta would like that even less.'

It was true that Jacinta Monday was particularly

passionate about Caro's freedom. Having been brought up in the strictest of circumstances herself, she was determined her daughter should not be similarly confined. Caro was allowed to roam all over the place. Across the river, up to Holborn, even as far as Camden Town. Passers-by would often stop and stare. It wasn't every day you saw a wiry girl and a ginger-eared rabbit bounding up and down London's busy thoroughfares.

'All right, then, just let me stay in the pub!' Caro pleaded. For all her fearlessness, Caro Monday did not like change. Yes, she loved her freedom, she loved to explore. But that was because the pub was always there to come home to afterwards. It was her anchor. She couldn't think of anything worse than being cast away into a stranger's home. She didn't understand why she couldn't just stay in Waterloo even though Ronnie wouldn't be there to look after her.

She nudged His Nibs back into his hutch, and watched as he made himself comfortable and started to munch on some fresh carrot tops.

'If Toby's allowed, why not me?'

Toby lived in the attic room at the top of the pub. He was employed to collect and wash the glasses and do heavy things, like unload the crates and change the beer barrels. In actual fact, he spent more time admiring his own reflection in the ancient spotted mirror in the saloon bar, or hanging around in the street, smoking and chatting with his friends. He didn't seem remotely interested in Caro and she wasn't remotely interested in him.

But just as Ronnie had decided to give him his marching orders, he'd come up trumps.

'Toby *won't* be on his own,' Ronnie explained. 'It's a stroke of luck his mother used to run a pub. She's going to mind this place for me. I can't ask her to look after you as well.'

'But, Ronnie! I don't *need* looking after. I can look after myself. And anyway, Mum is bound to get your telegram any day now!' wailed Caro. 'As soon as she does, she'll come home.'

But the trouble was, everything had happened so quickly: Ronnie's sister having the operation; Ronnie announcing she would have to leave the pub for a while so she could go and visit her.

They'd thought it would be OK because Mum would be home by then. But the first telegram had been sent a week ago, to the Manaus Opera House in the middle of the Amazon rainforest. The second had gone off a few days later, and then another one yesterday.

Neither Caro nor Ronnie could understand why they'd heard nothing back. Ronnie said *try not to worry*, but that was easier said than done.

'It won't be so bad, you'll see,' said Ronnie, drawing Caro close. Her pinafore was patterned with tiny violets and daisies. She smelled of cinnamon and nutmeg and her hug made Caro feel, for a moment, safe. But as quick as it had come, the moment passed. Ronnie was wrong. It *would* be bad. How could it not be when Caro couldn't remember a time without the woman who, in partnership with Jacinta, had looked after her since she was a baby.

Caro had heard the story so many times it had stitched itself into their family history: how, eleven years ago, caught out in the rain, Ronnie had taken shelter in the Sunset Club, in Soho.

How, once inside, time seemed to stop as Ronnie sat transfixed, watching Jacinta Monday whistle her way through her repertoire.

How, when the applause finally died away, Ronnie didn't leave with the rest of the audience, but went backstage to ask the whistler for an autograph.

And *that* was when she saw the baby: tiny, pink-cheeked, asleep in a drawer in Jacinta's dressing room, and ...

In one fell swoop, Ronnie fell in love with Caro just as much as she had with Jacinta.

The trio had been together ever since. They were a family and Caro called Ronnie her 'other mother'.

'Remember, Caro,' Ronnie was saying, back in the here and now, 'Great Aunt Mary has another ward as well – a boy called Albert – so you'll have company.'

Caro jerked back. She knew all about Great Aunt Mary: *Gam*, she called her in her head. Strict, cold-hearted, stuck in the Victorian age. She had been her mother's guardian until she was sixteen, at which point, unable to stand it any longer, Jacinta had run away.

Barely a word had been exchanged since. And now Caro couldn't understand why Ronnie was sending her to stay with someone her mother quite clearly detested.

'Why can't I stay with Horace?' she asked. She and Horace Braithwaite were best friends. They had known each other since they were three years old and had stuck together through thick and thin – a necessity at school, where they'd been picked on. Caro because she had two mums; Horace because his family were Bajan.

'You're different, be proud of it,' Ronnie and Jacinta had said.

'You're better than them, they'd better believe it,' said Mrs Braithwaite.

So Horace and Caro had banded up, fought their corner and, apart from by their sworn enemies, the Bully Boys, they weren't picked on any more.

Staying with Horace would be perfect, thought Caro. It made much more sense than being packed off to Hampstead.

But 'Mrs Braithwaite has her hands full with little Edwin,' said Ronnie. 'And you know very well there's not an inch of spare space.'

'I'd sleep on the floor!' burst out Caro. 'Or let me come with you! I can help look after your sister. I'll be good, I'll do anything you ask me to!'

'I wish I could say yes,' said Ronnie, frowning. 'But Marjorie really has been very poorly. Maybe when her condition improves...'

They both knew the real problem was Mr Marjorie. Marjorie's husband Harry was in the navy and had somehow organised to be on manoeuvres when his wife came out of hospital. It should be him looking after her while she was recuperating, not Ronnie, thought Caro.

Caro turned back to the hutch and stuck her finger through the chicken wire to tickle the rabbit's nose.

'Oh, Caro,' said Ronnie. 'Don't you think I've been through all the possibilities? I'm at my wits' end. If only Jacinta had come back when she was meant to, we wouldn't *be* in this pickle.'

Caro ignored her. It was more than a pickle. It was a catastrophe. 'Just you and me, then,' she said to His Nibs.

Ronnie gave an awkward cough.

Caro whirled round and saw that Ronnie's eyes had turned down at the corners, a sure sign that she was about to say something serious.

But what could be more serious than the fact that her sister was sick, that Jacinta Monday had gone missing, and that there would be no gym?

As realisation dawned, every bone in Caro's body seemed to crackle, and a whole host of butterflies inside her chest began to beat their wings. Jacinta had given His Nibs to Caro for a reason. To look after her when she was away. 'For extra love,' had been her actual words. And it had worked. When Caro was upset, His Nibs always calmed her. When she couldn't sleep, she would fetch him from his hutch and he would soothe her. How could she be expected to weather this change if they were to be separated? They'd never been separated before! Even on the few occasions when they'd been on holiday, he had been allowed to come too.

The thought of leaving him behind made Caro feel peculiarly dizzy and a bit sick.

'Don't tell me . . .' She could hardly get the words out. 'Am I not allowed to take him with me?'

'We can't expect your great-aunt to house a rabbit as well as you. How would you get his hutch there? It's too complicated. He'll be fine here; Toby can feed him—'

'That ignoramus!'

In the fading light, Caro Monday turned red, then white, then red again. Not only was she being sent to stay with someone who had made her mother miserable; she wasn't even allowed to take her one comfort, His Nibs, with her. She couldn't believe Ronnie was even thinking it. Didn't she understand that she wouldn't survive?

Angrily, she shoved past Ronnie, stomped through the pub, ignoring the surprised stares of the regulars, and slammed out of the front door.

'Got yer knickers in a twist, have ya?' said Toby, who was loitering outside.

'Oh, shut up,' said Caro. And in a blind rush, she ran through the narrow tangle of streets, up Waterloo Road, past the Rubbles, past the shot tower and across the stretch of green in front of the Royal Festival Hall – bright white against the soot-blackened city, its great glass windows casting huge puddles of light onto the River Thames.

The sky had darkened, the lamps had been lit, and specks of rain clung to the foggy air. Taking three at a time, Caro leapt up the steps to Hungerford Bridge. Below, the black waters of the river churned menacingly. To her left, a train screeched and wailed its way into Charing Cross. Above, the iron girders hulked like giant monsters. It was her place. The place she always came to when she was angry and upset. It was both terrible and wonderful at the same time.

Swiftly, Caro swung herself up so that one foot was planted on top of the railing and the other was jammed into the wire fence separating the narrow walkway from the railway track. Unlike His Nibs, who was afraid of heights, Caro Monday loved to climb. One day, she was going to travel the world just like her mother. Maybe as a gymnast. Or a tightrope walker. Or someone who could scale whole buildings using just her hands and feet.

But how could she do that if she didn't get the chance to practise? And practising meant she needed a gym. Throwing her head back, Caro howled, her voice in mad competition with the din of the train, the curl of her breath disappearing into the murky air.

No one could hear her. The city workers, who thronged the bridge during the rush hour, wouldn't be back until Monday morning. *They* weren't being sent away, holiday plans ruined and deprived of the company of their dear darling rabbit. The train rumbled past, clanking and sparking, and then it was gone and on the opposite side of the river Big Ben chimed six, a kind of finale, each *dong* thudding deep inside Caro's chest.

Tucking her legs over the railing, Caro swung upside down, so that she could see everything the wrong way up: Waterloo Bridge, the curve of the Thames, the dome of St Paul's.

'Caro!'

Caro flipped back up into a sitting position. It was Horace, dashing up the steps, jumping elegantly over the puddles, dressed in his school uniform even though it was a Sunday. Of course, on Horace, it didn't look like a school uniform. It looked like a suit, a particularly dashing suit, with a sage green handkerchief peeping out of his top pocket and a matching tie. Horace wanted to be a fashion designer when he grew up, like his hero, 'the little prince of fashion', Yves Saint Laurent. At twenty-three, Saint Laurent was the world's youngest couturier, famous for producing six hundred drawings in fifteen days. Horace was always sketching nineteen to the dozen too. Caro wouldn't be surprised if he could produce six hundred drawings in *seven* days.

Caro jumped down from her perch, landing on the balls of her feet with her arms outstretched and her chest concave, like a Russian gymnast. Horace pushed his black-framed glasses back onto his nose and looked anxiously back the way he had come.

'What? Are the Bully Boys after you again?'

The Bully Boys were in the same year as Caro and Horace at South Square Secondary. They had hard faces and mean eyes and they were always starting fights with anyone who wasn't like them.

'They tried to get me,' said Horace. 'But I was too quick for them.' He put his fists up and danced on the spot like the greatest boxer of all time, Sugar Ray Robinson.

Caro knew Horace could fight his own corner. Still, she would've punched those ignoramuses right in their faces if she'd been there.

'Anyway, forget about them. Mrs Rudd sent me to get you,' said Horace. 'Says it's important. Says you have to come home right away.'

* * *

Back at the pub, Ronnie was waiting with Caro's best supper ever, 'the three-potato special', a plate piled high with mashed potato, roast potatoes and chips. Caro eyed the plate uneasily. Potatoes were Caro's favourite. Having three varieties all at once meant bad news.

Caro sat down at the table with a thump and picked up her fork. She was dimly aware that Ronnie had her coat on. And that her suitcase was by the door.

On the kitchen counter, the radio crackled. Something about an elderly lady who had just been burgled. 'They took my best soup tureen!' she said in a frail, wavery voice. 'It was a family heirloom!'

Ronnie clicked the radio off and sat down opposite Caro, regarding her solemnly.

'What's going on?' asked Caro. 'You've packed already? And why have you got your coat on? I thought you weren't going until the day after tomorrow!'

'I'm so sorry, Caro love, but the doctor phoned while you were out. They're ready to discharge Marjorie, and with Harry still away I've got no choice but to go immediately. I've shut the pub early and I'm catching the last train.'

Caro set her fork down with a crash. At least if

Ronnie had stuck to the original plan and left the day after tomorrow, there might've been the tiniest chance that Jacinta would've turned up in the nick of time.

But now?! It was really happening. She was actually going to have to go to this unknown great-aunt tomorrow!

A horrible feeling of dread crept over her.

'I still don't understand how you can ... I mean, Mum ... when she finds out ...' She could barely string the words together, she was so upset. Ronnie didn't seem to understand how terrible she was feeling. How scared she was and how frightening it was even *thinking* about being away from the pub.

'Your mum's stubborn ...' said Ronnie. She had a funny look on her face. Almost as if she were hiding something.

'Stubborn?!' cried Caro disbelievingly. 'But of course she is. Great Aunt Mary was awful to her, that's what she *always* said!'

'When we could squeeze any information out of her,' responded Ronnie quietly.

Caro picked up a chip and then put it down again. She wasn't remotely hungry. Even for potatoes.

It was true that Jacinta didn't like to talk about

certain things. In fact, mainly two things: The War and Great Aunt Mary. She always said, 'Don't waste your breath,' and changed the subject, and that was that. Caro and Ronnie had come to learn they were subjects best avoided.

'Thing is,' said Ronnie, 'what with Marjorie being ill and your mum going AWOL, it started me thinking. Family *is* important.'

'But we *are* a family!' said Caro. What was Ronnie getting at?

Ronnie met Caro's gaze and held it steadily. 'If anything were to happen to your mum – not that it will! – but just say it did ... maybe it's time to make amends ... with her family. *Your* family.'

'What do you mean, if anything happens to her?' Caro felt a chilly prickle of fear. What was Ronnie talking about? 'She'll be home soon. She's just got into one of her scrapes!'

Ronnie stood up. Kissed Caro's forehead. 'I'm sure you're right,' she said. 'But in the meantime, Toby's mum will be here first thing in the morning and Great Aunt Mary is expecting you in the afternoon. Can you manage? You'll need to pack a case. Take Jacinta's old one. And there's money in the teapot for your tube fare ...'

Despite the practical instructions, Caro had never seen Ronnie look so worried. In fact, it was more than worry, it was distress. A deeper frown had appeared than had ever been there before, and the corners of her eyes were so droopy it did something painful to Caro's heart.

'I'm sorry, Caro. We're just going to have to make the best of it. Do you think you can do that?'

'Yes,' she said, 'I suppose so.' Despite all her protestations, she didn't want to add to Ronnie's difficulties.

'And you promise to try and be polite to your great-aunt? Not cause any trouble?'

Was that an actual tear squeezing its way out of Ronnie's right eye? But Ronnie *never* cried.

In a flash Caro jumped up and clutched her other mother in a fierce hug. She wouldn't be selfish. She couldn't. 'Sorry, sorry, sorry! I promise I won't cause any trouble. I'll be polite. You go to Marjorie. I'll go to Hampstead and before we know it, Mum will be home.'

Chapter Two

It was an odd night, all alone in the pub, without the comfort of Ronnie's steady snoring.

Toby had gone straight out after Ronnie had left and hadn't been seen since. He'd been out an awful lot lately, thought Caro. Maybe that would change when his mum arrived.

Caro stayed up late, watching *her* mum's favourite programme, *Barry Bucknell's Do-It-Yourself*, and then in bed, tried not to listen to the pub's creaks and groans. She knew perfectly well they were just the familiar sounds of a tired old building, but all of a sudden they seemed to have taken on a rather sinister tinge.

Unsurprisingly, she couldn't sleep. Her head was

full of thoughts and questions about tomorrow. She tried to picture herself turning up in Hampstead, with her mum's old suitcase, but she couldn't hold the picture still. All she could think about was, what had this Great Aunt Mary done to make Jacinta run away? Was she actually as cruel as Jacinta said? She must have done something really unspeakable if – even now – her mother could hardly bear to talk about her.

And why had Ronnie said that thing about families? About making amends? In case something *happened* to Mum, had been her actual words. But nothing could happen to her, could it? Not to her wonderful mum. Jacinta Monday, world-famous whistler, who travelled all over the globe to perform in theatres and concert halls. Jacinta Monday who could whistle anything: birdsong, whole arias, all the hymns, symphonies and sonatas.

At last, Caro smiled into the dark. She couldn't whistle a *thing*. Or click her fingers. Ronnie and Jacinta would egg her on to try and then collapse in fits of giggles at her efforts.

But where *was* her mother?

It wasn't the first time she had disappeared.

Once, in Moscow, she had boarded the Trans-Siberian Express to Vladivostok instead of the sleeper train to Berlin and hadn't been seen or heard of for ten whole days. Another time, she'd gone on an expedition deep into the Amazon jungle, got lost and – until she was found by a forgotten tribe – been unable to make contact for an entire week.

Ronnie called these episodes 'scrapes', but Caro and Jacinta preferred to call them adventures. *Spectacular* adventures. Caro crossed her fingers. She was almost one hundred per cent sure that her mother was having one right now.

Just... why did she have to have one when they were meant to be building the gym? *And* when Ronnie had to go on her emergency mission to look after Marjorie. It really was the worst possible time to get into a scrape.

And when she *did* get back, she'd be so cross to find that Ronnie had sent Caro to stay with Gam. Jacinta had always been very clear. She didn't want anything to do with her aunt.

Caro turned over and drew her knees up to her chest. Tomorrow morning, before she left, she'd meet Horace in the Rubbles. She pictured the dumped car with the yellowy foam exploding out of the red-leather seats; the den they'd made out of old blackboards and planks of wood; the tyres to swing from, and the dustbin lids and all the other stuff that nobody wanted. She loved the

Rubbles: half bombsite, half junk yard, full of stuff to build with, and no grown-ups to bother you.

There was bound to be nothing *half* like the Rubbles in Hampstead. And even if there was, it wouldn't be the same without Horace.

She would come back every day. It was only half an hour on the tube. They could still *try* and build the gym on their own. Even if it was bound to be a bit ramshackle. It would be a surprise for Jacinta when she got back.

Outside, a train rumbled past. Caro flung herself from bed and peered through the window. Her bedroom looked onto the railway arches and she watched the tail end of the train disappear into the velvety night air. Below, she could just about make out the long shadow of the rabbit hutch. His Nibs would comfort her. *He'd* stop her mind racing. Grabbing her dressing gown, she padded downstairs and into the yard.

'Come on, sonny-boy,' she said, heaving the rabbit out and holding him over her shoulder like a giant baby. He snuffled contentedly. When he'd first arrived he'd been small enough to fit into her cupped hands – hard to believe now that he was so huge. They thudded back up the stairs. Ronnie always said that for all Caro's gymnastics, she had the grace of an elephant.

Mind you, there wasn't a chance of doing anything gracefully when you were carrying a heffalump like His Nibs.

In bed, Caro stroked the rabbit's ears and slowly a plan started to form. A plan that made her feel much, much better. Now that Ronnie had gone, she wouldn't know if Caro decided to take the rabbit to Hampstead, would she? And if His Nibs came with her, she might – just might – be able to bear it, being away from the pub, and Mum and Ronnie and Horace. True, Caro had made Ronnie a promise not to cause any trouble. Well, if she had His Nibs by her side, she would be much less likely to. She'd have to keep him a secret of course. This Gam didn't sound much like the animal-loving type.

Downstairs, the front door slammed. At last. It must be Toby. She could hear him crashing around in the saloon bar and as he passed her room, she heard him muttering to himself.

'I'll show 'em. A black leather jacket; a nice little sports car; furs and diamonds...'

Caro snorted. Toby obviously had more of an imagination than she gave him credit for. If you wanted those things you had to work hard for them, not be the sort of person who did the least that was expected of him!

Carefully, she nudged His Nibs who – as usual – was taking up far more space than his fair share of the pillow.

'Don't worry,' she whispered. 'I'll never abandon *you*.'

His Nibs twitched his nose in reply and Caro felt a wash of calm sweep over her.

And at last, she slept.

* * *

The next day His Nibs and Caro had breakfast together. There was just enough space on the kitchen table for the rabbit to munch his hay and for Caro's plate of toast and jam. She was about to wash up her plate when Toby sauntered in. He had put some greasy stuff into his hair and a new spot bloomed on his chin.

'Mrs Standing... Emerald... I mean, Ma, is held up. She said to look after yourself and keep the pub closed today. No harm done.'

Caro and His Nibs looked at Toby agog. No harm done? Apart from yesterday when emergency matters had forced an early closing, Ronnie had never had a day off in her life. Caro imagined all the regulars shuffling up to the entrance and looking baffled and befuddled at the closed doors. That wouldn't do. It wouldn't do at all.

'No need to look like that,' said Toby crossly. He had a funny way of talking, as if he always had a blocked-up nose, which made it hard to take him seriously. 'It ain't the end of the world.' He dug his comb out of his pocket and swung through the door into the saloon bar, where in front of the old spotted mirror he began the laborious process of perfecting his quiff.

His Nibs and Caro stared at each other. His Nibs blinked first and resumed his hay chewing. Caro got a pen and paper out of the odds-and-ends drawer.

> Very sorry, pub shut today.
> Open again tomorrow.

She was just pinning it to the front door when Toby emerged, squinting in the bright morning light.

'Got some business to attend to,' he said in a way that made Caro think he was trying to be as mysterious as possible. He stuck his hands in his pockets and swaggered off down the street. Honestly, thought Caro, he thinks he's so important now his mum is going to be running things. He wasn't even very good at swaggering. She and Horace were much better.

'I won't be here when you get back,' she yelled after his disappearing figure. 'And you don't need to worry about feeding His Nibs, I'm taking him with me.'

Caro spent a short while in the saloon bar practising walking on her hands while His Nibs hopped around her in circles. She turned the radio on and listened to a snatch of news – something about the Snakes yet again.

The Snakes were dangerous criminals suspected of a recent spate of thefts across the capital. It was probably them who had stolen that elderly lady's soup tureen she'd heard about on the radio yesterday. Now, a brisk-sounding reporter was interviewing an ex-gang member called Trevor.

Trevor described how the Snakes had chopped off his finger because they thought he was giving away trade secrets. They'd wrapped it up in newspaper and sent it to his mum in the post as a warning. Caro imagined the dismembered finger tumbling out, all grey and bloody. Trevor said his mum had fainted with the shock of it. Caro would've screamed the house down if that had happened to her.

'Cross them at yer peril,' Trevor told the reporter.

Caro shuddered and tuned the radio to a more cheerful station. That was more like it: Buddy Holly. 'That'll be the day-yay-yay when I die,' Caro sang along.

Then she grabbed a shopping bag and some money from the teapot, and left His Nibs snuffling happily along to the music in the saloon.

In Lower Marsh, she bought two iced buns and two sacks of hay. Then she made her way to the greengrocer's where she collected a huge bag of carrot tops and a load of cauliflower leaves.

'There's some peelings in there, from last night's dinner,' said the grocer. 'And how about these apples? Bit bruised, but cut off the bad bits and they should be fine.'

Back in the pub, Caro wriggled under Ronnie's bed in search of the suitcase, but the only things under there were a thick layer of dust and several old copies of the *Practical Householder*.

Caro sniffed and tried once again not to think about her mother's whereabouts, or about the gym she and Horace were going to have to build on their own. The important thing was to find the suitcase. Where was it? Then she remembered. Last year she and her mum had gone to Swan and Edgar to choose a brand new one. They'd picked out a bright red case with gold buckles. Afterwards they'd gone to the café on the top floor for marmalade tart.

The old suitcase would be in the cellar, tucked

amongst the beer barrels, along with all the other ancient stuff that was no longer in use but too precious to throw out. It was a handsome thing – chestnut leather, stamped with all the places Jacinta had been to: Vienna, Rome, Istanbul, and lots of other distant destinations too faded and torn to read.

Caro clattered down the cellar steps, grabbed the suitcase and ran back up, fast. She didn't like the cellar. It was dark and musty and had ominous corners. Only last week Ronnie had reported hearing scrabbling sounds and Caro had convinced herself it was full of sharp-toothed rats.

When she had packed, Caro set off for the Rubbles with the iced buns and the apples. Apples were always useful in an emergency.

Horace was already there, reading a battered old copy of *Vogue* with his feet up on the back seat of the dumped car. He was wearing brown lace-up shoes polished to such a shine you could almost see your face in them, and bright pink socks with a green stripe at the top.

'What?' he said. 'What's the matter, Caro?' They knew each other so well, he could tell just by looking at her that something was wrong.

'Ronnie had to leave yesterday, which means I've got

to go to my Great Aunt Mary's house this afternoon,' she said glumly.

'But what about the gym?' asked Horace, looking just as indignant as Caro had felt yesterday. She knew he'd understand. He seemed to be the only person in the world who did. 'You know we worked out you've only got four more years of holidays before you leave school to practise your skills!'

He was right. They'd done the sums together, in the back of Horace's sketchbook. Thirteen weeks (six weeks' summer holidays, two weeks each at Easter and Christmas, three one-week half-terms) times four years equalled fifty-two weeks' practice. Each week was absolutely vital. Caro was already twelve and her great plan was to be a performer by the time she was sixteen.

'I know!' wailed Caro, 'but mum's not back to help and...'

'It's only half an hour on the tube though, isn't it?' interrupted Horace. 'You could...'

'...come back every day to visit?' said Caro. Great minds think alike, she thought.

'We can *try* to build it on our own,' said Horace thoughtfully. 'Or at least make a start. Your great-aunt will probably be pleased to have you off her hands. Especially as it sounds like she doesn't much like children.'

That was true. But even though that should've made Caro feel better, it didn't.

'What else?' asked Horace, because he knew his friend and he could tell there was something else troubling her.

Caro hung over one of the tyre swings, resting her tummy on the rubber so that her legs and arms swung free.

'Ronnie said something really odd yesterday,' she started. 'About the importance of families and making amends and …' A horrible thought suddenly struck her and it was so shocking she blurted it out. 'What if Mum doesn't come back and I have to live with this Great Aunt Mary for the rest of my life?'

'That's not going to happen, Caro!' Horace exclaimed. 'Your mum's just off having one of her adventures. She'll be back soon.'

'D'you really think so?' she said. How could he be so sure? Did he really believe that? The voice of reason, Jacinta always said about Horace. He was the sensible one, mostly.

'And just say she doesn't come back,' he continued, because Horace was good at looking at a subject from all angles, 'although I'm sure she will – then why wouldn't Ronnie just carry on looking after you?'

Caro didn't answer because she wasn't sure what the answer was. Would Ronnie be able to look after her? They called themselves a family ... but strictly speaking ... well, Caro knew there were laws about it. Marriage, blood relations, all that. Was Great Aunt Mary the type to follow the law?

'Caro!' Horace was clicking his fingers, trying to get her attention. 'Look what I fetched from home!'

He disappeared behind the car and came back moments later with an enormous pram, boasting huge silver wheels and a capacious hood.

'Ta da! It's been in the back yard for ages – that's why it's a bit rusty. Mum's saving it to pass on to Aunty Sandra when she has her baby.'

'*Is* Aunty Sandra having a baby?' asked Caro. Aunty Sandra was a singer in the Sunset Club and she could hit a G over a high C which meant she could sing three whole octaves. Sometimes she and Caro's mum duetted together, giving impromptu performances at the pub. That was how Caro and Horace's families had got to know each other.

'Not yet,' said Horace. 'Says she's got to find a man first. So, no one's going to need this pram for a while.' He trundled it back and forth and then he demonstrated how you could have the hood up, or down, like a pram salesman. The wheels squeaked noisily as they turned.

'You saying I can borrow it?' asked Caro.

'That's why I fetched it!' said Horace. 'Thought it might come in useful if you need to keep His Nibs a secret from your great-aunt.'

'Horace, you are the brilliantest friend,' she said. She could use the pram as a sort of makeshift hutch. Plus, His Nibs hated travelling on the tube. He would feel much safer tucked up inside it.

'*And* I made something for you. It's your lucky day.'

Horace was holding out a brown paper package and waving it about enticingly. He was always making things. He had his own sewing box and everyone gave him their old clothes so that he could unpick them and turn them into something new. Last year he'd made Jacinta a turquoise cocktail dress for a performance at the Royal Albert Hall, and Aunty Sandra had made him promise that if she ever got married, he would design her wedding dress.

Inside the package was a swingy cape fashioned out of chestnut brown velvet.

'It's a *travelling* cape,' said Horace. 'I know it's only

eleven stops on the tube, but . . . I made it out of the old sitting-room curtains. D'you like it?'

'I love it!' said Caro admiring the neat stitching and the gold ribbon trim. She swung the cape over her shoulders and did up the little gilt clasp under her chin. It was exactly the same shade of brown as Jacinta's old suitcase. It fitted perfectly and flipped satisfyingly when she moved.

'Hungry?' she asked.

'Starving,' he said. And so Caro dug in the bag of now rather squashed iced buns and handed one over.

While they munched their buns, they talked. They loved to talk. They could talk for hours. The subject today was the circus Horace had been to see with his dad the day before. He was just getting to the bit about an acrobat called Tomaz Topaz, who wore turquoise sequins and performed death-defying feats on the tightrope, and Caro was firing questions left, right and centre about his balancing technique, when on the other side of the Rubbles three figures emerged from a mound of scrap metal and timber.

'Uh oh,' said Caro.

'The Bully Boys,' groaned Horace. There was no mistaking their long jackets and skinny ties and the way they ran their fingers through their greasy mops of hair. Acting like they owned the place, as usual.

'Quick,' said Caro. 'Behind the den.'

Hidden from sight, Caro grabbed a couple of dustbin lids, passed one to Horace and kept one for herself. They made good shields.

They could hear the Bully Boys' rough shouts and laughter. They never passed up the chance to have a good fight.

'We haven't got any ammunition,' whispered Horace.

'We have,' said Caro, waving the emergency bag of bruised apples at him.

'We saw ya,' yelled the biggest one. His name was Frank and his mum worked in the tobacconist's by the station.

'Chicken!' yelled the middle one, Stanley, all taut, wiry muscles with the manner of a bull terrier.

'Sissy!' parroted the third one, Carl, who was as scrawny as he was short, but more than made up for it in venom. Just because Horace liked drawing and making clothes, *Sissy* was their favourite insult, which showed how stupid they were.

'No-brains!' yelled Horace, grabbing a handful of apples and leaping up to take aim. He was a good shot and the first apple whizzed straight through the air hitting Frank squarely on the forehead. The second shot pounded, BAM, into Stanley's chest.

And the third one made direct contact with Carl's Adam's apple.

Before the Bully Boys could collect themselves, three more apples came hurtling through the air, this time expertly dispatched by Caro.

And then there was a battle of apples and sticks and stones, the shields clanging as they took the brunt of the missiles. Steadily, the enemy advanced. The biggest one brandishing a large stick; the middle one preparing a sling out of a dirty handkerchief crammed with wizened conkers; the shortest one with his fists up and a terrifying scowl.

Caro and Horace fought back with all their might, Caro drawing on all the frustration of the last few days and directing it at Frank and Stanley and Carl. The tension that had been eating away at her bubbled up and spilled over, making her stronger and braver and unwilling to back down.

'Caro,' muttered Horace when they had hurled the last of the apples. 'What next?'

Out of the corner of her eye Caro spied the remains of a fire they'd made a few days earlier. In a sudden rush, she kicked out at the mound of charred wood and cinders, using her heel for added impact. A great billowing cloud of dusty black ash filled the air, and – yes! It was as if a curtain had come down between them and the enemy, and then they were off, dragging the pram behind them, rattling and bumping their way to a hole in the wall hidden by brambles.

By the time the dust had settled, the Bully Boys, still coughing and spluttering, finally found the hole themselves. But by then their prey were streets away, sauntering up Belvedere Road, busily making plans for the construction of Caro's gym in the Rubbles.

Chapter Three

His Nibs detested the London Underground. It was loud and juddery, and as the train rattled its way from south to north, his muscles tensed, his ears drooped until they lay flat, and no amount of stroking and gentle scratching from Caro could make it better. It was a relief when they finally reached their stop.

But as Caro turned into the cobbled street that led down to the heath, her legs turned leaden. She felt as if there were weights attached to her feet. Her resolve – buoyed up by her decision to travel back to Waterloo every single day to see Horace and build the gym – crumbled. The fluttering feeling rushed back into her chest with a vengeance. She was convinced that she couldn't possibly take one more step.

There was a bench at the top of Flask Walk and she sat down with a bump, gripping the handle of the pram with such force that her knuckles turned white.

Opposite the bench was a news stand. The *Daily News*, the *Hampstead News*, the *Illustrated London News*, all jostling for space, their headlines jumping out at her: 'Snakes seemingly unstoppable.' 'Latest thefts in Highgate, Hampstead and Kensington.' '"Guard your antiques" advise Scotland Yard.'

'My word, he's a fine fellow.'

In her panic, Caro hadn't noticed the gentleman bundled up in several coats sitting at the other end of the bench. He had a long reddish-brown beard and at his side was a large stick with a sack slung on the end of it. He was talking about His Nibs, who was sitting up in the pram and peering all around with great interest.

'Yes, he is, isn't he?' she replied, struggling to keep her voice level. It was the kindness, maybe, in the man's voice that made her feel suddenly tearful. Only eleven stops on the tube, Horace had said. But already, Waterloo and everyone she loved most felt like a world away.

'Everything all right?' asked the man.

'Sort of,' said Caro even though it wasn't.

'You've had a hard day.' A statement, not a question.

The man leaned down to pull up a clump of chickweed that was bursting through the cracks in the pavement and handed it to His Nibs.

'There you go, old fellow,' he said.

His Nibs attacked the chickweed gratefully.

'Tomorrow will probably be better,' said the gentleman. 'And if not, the day after that. Things keep moving. Nothing stays as it is, that's what I always tell myself.'

'Yes,' said Caro. The gentleman's words were oddly comforting. She supposed he was right. After all, tomorrow was one day sooner to Jacinta coming home and Ronnie coming back.

She looked at her wristwatch. Nearly five o'clock. Ronnie had said Gam was expecting her in the afternoon.

'We'd better go,' she said, a little of her resolve returning. She stood up and turned the pram in the direction of the heath.

'Courage!' said the man. He said it the French way – *cou-rarrrge* – and at the same time he gave a sort of salute. Caro saluted back, and as she did so, she felt her chest lift a little and her shoulders go back.

'It was nice to meet you,' she said, and she genuinely meant it. 'Thanks for the chickweed.'

'A pleasure,' said the man. 'And by the way, the name's Victor. I do hope we shall meet again.'

* * *

Gam's house was a large red-brick villa facing the heath, all dark windows and creeping ivy. In front was a gravel drive, its edges shrouded in a thicket of bushes. It was a solemn-looking house. On the gate was screwed an iron plaque: Heath View.

Glancing up at the blank windows, Caro pushed the pram a little way along the drive. Ronnie had said not to bring the rabbit. What if Gam was so cross about it that she telephoned Ronnie straight away and told her what Caro had done? Ronnie would be so disappointed. Caro could almost hear her saying, 'Caro! You failed at the first hurdle. Didn't I tell you not to cause any trouble?'

In a flash, Caro knew what she had to do and, executing a quick right turn, pushed the pram into the depths of the deepest, darkest, shrub.

'Stay there,' she whispered as commandingly as she was able. His Nibs's little black eyes met hers trustingly. 'I'll be back to get you when the coast is clear. All right?'

He was a loyal rabbit and he twitched his one ginger ear and one white ear in agreement.

'What on earth are you doing, girl?'

Caro whirled round, trying hard not to look guilty. The front door had opened and a forbidding-looking figure in a long, droopy black dress stood on the threshold. She was leaning on a green silk umbrella as though it were a walking stick. Now she raised the umbrella and pointed it at Caro.

'Nothing,' said Caro, darting away from the bush, adjusting her cape and picking up her suitcase. Gam looked exactly like she had expected her to, her expression cold, her attire giving the impression that – just as Jacinta had said – she was stuck in the Victorian age. '*Cou-rarrge*,' Caro said to herself, echoing the gentleman Victor's words. Then taking a deep breath, she approached the house and mounted the front steps.

'I take it you are Caroline Monday,' said Great Aunt Mary, giving her a piercing look.

'It's Caro,' said Caro stoutly. 'I won't answer to anything else.' Ronnie had said she must be polite. But didn't she also always say start how you mean to carry on?

Great Aunt Mary's eyebrows shot up, almost disappearing under her black lace cap.

'Well, I never! Answering back already,' she said in an aggrieved tone. 'I can see you've not been taught your manners and I cannot say I am surprised. Anyone raised in a public house must be expected to have picked up – how should I put it? – rough ways.'

Caro glowered, but she followed her great-aunt inside the house and waited while she bellowed, 'Marks, please come at once! You are never here when I need you!' She had a surprisingly booming voice for such a gaunt figure.

A clatter of steps heralded the arrival of a young woman. She had a curtain of black hair and a fringe so long she could barely see out of it. She could not have been much older than twenty.

'Sorry, Mary,' she said. 'I was just making the tea.'

'Tea! At this hour? Marks, how many times do I have to tell you that tea is traditionally served between three and four? Take this young smidge up to the nursery, make the necessary introductions and then show her to her room.'

The elderly lady turned to Caro and regarded her with a steady eye. 'Marks is my "help", not a maid-of-all-work, so don't even *think* of ordering her about.'

Caro nodded OK, even though she had never heard of a maid-of-all-work, and even if she had, she would never have dreamed of ordering her about. It sounded like a job from a bygone age.

'Now, I shall see you in the dining room at seven o'clock sharp for supper. Marks, *do* try not to burn anything.'

As Great Aunt Mary disappeared into her lair, Marks grabbed Caro's suitcase and, balancing it on top of her head, proceeded up the stairs. Caro noticed she had a streak of blue paint on her trousers and something that looked like a paintbrush sticking out of her hair.

'D'you live here too?' she asked, hurrying to keep up. Marks was taking the stairs two at a time.

'Your great-aunt lets me live in the room at the top of the house,' said Marks. 'See, I had a big barney with my family last year 'cause they wanted me to go to secretarial college and *I* want to be an artist. Some people compare my work to Jackson Pollock, you know.'

Caro didn't know. She didn't have the faintest idea who Jackson Pollock was.

'Anyway,' carried on Marks, oblivious to Caro's ignorance, 'I answered the ad in the newsagent's. In exchange for doing some cooking and cleaning,

I get to live here rent-free and I can paint whenever I want.'

They had reached the third-floor landing and Marks kicked a door open with her foot, nodding at Caro to step inside.

It was a large room looking out onto the back garden, and on the floor, in front of a gas fire, knelt a slight-looking boy surrounded by a vast array of knitting needles and wool. He glanced up, gave a huge sniff and wiped his nose on his sleeve.

'Cheer up, Albie, the world's still turning,' said Marks. 'This is Caro. Be nice, please, and show her to her room.'

'Why can't you?' asked Albie.

That wasn't very welcoming, thought Caro. In fact, it was downright rude.

'*Please*, Albie. I've got a shepherd's pie to put in the oven *and* I've got to use the last of the blue before it goes dry...'

The door closed and they both listened as Marks thundered her way up the stairs to her room above. Caro pressed her lips together tight. Charming! It was as if Gam and Marks couldn't wait to get rid of her. They'd certainly been quick enough about dumping her with this sorry-looking little fellow. Well, she wasn't going to be the one to get the ball rolling. She thought she could probably manage without any conversation, thank you very much.

'What are *you* doing here?' asked Albie eventually, turning back to his knitting needles. Well. It seemed he didn't care very much about her either. It didn't matter. She wasn't here to make friends. And it looked like that would suit everyone just fine.

'I didn't *choose* to come – my other mother Ronnie made me,' said Caro. 'As soon as my mum comes home, I'll be gone.'

'You've got *two* mums?' said Albie. *That* had got his attention. It usually did.

'Yeah, and what're you gonna do about it?' asked Caro combatively. She was used to people thinking two mums instead of one was a bit unusual, and she wasn't about to let a little boy get all high and mighty about it. Most people's eyes popped when she told them. 'Get used to it,' Jacinta would say.

'I was only asking,' said Albie in a wounded tone, and sniffed again.

'What's that?' asked Caro, nodding at the tangle of knitting needles and wool.

'Just making stuff,' he said. 'I found a box of them in the attic. Size-thirteen wooden ones are best. They're strong enough to—'

'Aren't you meant to be showing me to my room?' Caro interrupted. His face, which had become a little more animated when he'd been explaining about the knitting needles, closed up again. Still, Caro thought, it was probably best not to encourage him, seeing as she wasn't planning on hanging around.

Albie carefully laid the knitting needles aside and got to his feet. 'This way,' he said meekly.

Caro followed Albie along the landing to a room at the front of the house. It was a small, pretty room, with pale green walls and a yellow quilt on the bed. She couldn't help wondering if this might have been her mum's room when *she'd* lived here. Was this where Jacinta had practised her whistling? Had she stared out at exactly the same view when she'd been planning her escape aged sixteen?

Caro pushed the curtains aside. It was almost dusk but she could just about make out the loom of the shrub that concealed His Nibs. Beyond that lay the gate and then, across the road, the boundless heath. She crossed her fingers and hoped that the rabbit would stay tucked up inside the pram. Rabbits disliked change, that was a fact, so she was banking on him staying put and resisting exploration.

'What's out there?' asked Albie. Caro jumped. She

hadn't realised he was hovering right behind her.

'Don't creep up on me like that!' said Caro crossly, stepping away from the window. How did she know he wasn't a snoop? A tattletale? Best not say anything about His Nibs for now.

Albie was still carrying a knitting needle and now he started to tap out a rhythm on the wooden bedframe. The tune sounded much jollier than he looked. He had a narrow face and a pinched expression.

His eyes followed her as she unbuckled her suitcase and began dividing her belongings between the chest of drawers and the large wardrobe.

'Why are *you* living here?' she asked, seeing as he didn't seem to be going anywhere. She thought Ronnie might've mentioned the reason, but she couldn't remember what it was.

'My parents died,' he said. 'In a car accident. A bad one. There weren't any other relatives. And Mrs Monday was Dad's godmother.'

'Oh!' said Caro. She didn't know what else to say. Ronnie definitely hadn't mentioned *that*. It sounded awful.

'Anyway,' said Albie after a short silence, 'it's better than an orphanage. Or boarding school. Even if she does keep getting awful nannies to look after me.'

'Nannies?' echoed Caro. She had a vision of Mary Poppins swooping in with an umbrella to rival Gam's green silk one, and a carpet bag.

'That's what *she* calls them,' said Albie. 'But they're just ordinary ladies who don't even seem to *like* children very much. They answer the adverts she puts up in the newsagent's and then they come and boss me about. What's this?'

He was kneeling down, his head in Caro's suitcase, and now he turned, holding up a small package wrapped in newspaper and tied with string. 'Presents?'

His pinched little face looked hopeful. You couldn't help feeling a bit sorry for the poor thing, Caro thought. Orphaned then sent to live with Gam, and then subjected to a string of bossy nannies. Still, she hadn't asked him to help her unpack, nor should he be touching her things.

'Hand it over,' she said brusquely. She took the package from Albie and turned it over in her hands. Had Ronnie put it in there as a leaving present? It was doubtful. She hadn't even remembered to tell Caro that the suitcase had been moved to the cellar.

'Where d'you find it?' she asked.

'In there.' Albie was pointing to a zipped

compartment in the lining of the suitcase that Caro hadn't noticed before.

Carefully, Caro untied the string and peeled away the newspaper wrapping. Inside was a painting. It was small, about the size of a postcard, and gilt-framed. It was the prettiest painting Caro had ever seen, of a bird, all speckly brown, with a small crest, pale breast and white-tipped feathers. The bird was perched on a branch littered with dark-pink blossom and there were patches of pale-blue sky in the background.

'Just a boring old painting,' said Albie, disappointed.

'It's not boring, it's beautiful!' said Caro. What did he know? He was just a little kid. Horace would be much more appreciative. He knew all about art. He was always going to the big museums with his sketch pad. She wished he was here now so she could show it to him.

Maybe it *was* a present. Jacinta must have brought it back from one of her travels and forgotten to give it to her.

Down in the hall, a clock chimed seven.

'Supper time,' said Albie anxiously. 'Come on, we mustn't be late. She doesn't like it.'

Caro thought of the stern figure with the green silk umbrella waiting for them downstairs. What would happen if they *were* late? Would they be sent to bed without any supper? She wondered if Albie had always been so timid, or if it was living with Gam that had made him this way.

Caro turned to him. 'Are you afraid of her?'

'No!' said Albie crossly, twirling the knitting needle like a drum baton.

'OK, OK,' said Caro, vowing to herself that however horrid Gam turned out to be, she would never be cowed by her like timid little Albie.

'Come on!' said Albie. He was already out of the door.

'All right, coming,' said Caro, and, shoving the painting back into the suitcase, she steeled herself and followed Albie downstairs to the dining room.

Chapter Four

Downstairs, Great Aunt Mary and her umbrella were waiting for them. There was no sign of Marks.

The dining room stretched the entire length of the house. At one end, glass-paned double doors opened straight onto a back lawn. At the other end, a window looked out onto the gravel drive and the dark bushes in which His Nibs was concealed.

'Gracious,' Gam pronounced as they clattered into the room, 'I never heard such a racket! It's like the storming of the Bastille down here.'

She was still dressed in her droopy black, and her mouth was set in a thin, disapproving line.

'So, you've met this flibbertigibbet,' she said, nodding at Albie. 'I hope he has been polite and showed you to your room. You should have everything you need. Tell me if you've not.'

'Everything's fine, thank you,' said Caro stiffly. She wanted to go home, that's what she really wanted; she wanted Jacinta and Ronnie and life back to normal but there was no point in saying so.

Marks had left a steaming shepherd's pie on the table and a note informing them to look in the refrigerator for pudding. Albie opened the fridge door immediately. 'Ugh!' he said. 'Blancmange, with skin on it!'

There was a bit of life in him then, thought Caro.

'I heard that,' yelled a distant voice.

After a long remonstration, during which the umbrella was pointed and Great Aunt Mary delivered a tiresome lecture on being thankful for what you are given, they all sat down, Great Aunt Mary at the head of the table, her umbrella hooked on the back of her chair, Caro and Albie either side.

'Albert, will you *please* blow your nose?' said Great Aunt Mary. 'Caroline, *why* is your mouth hanging open? It looks *most* unbecoming.'

'I said to call me Caro!' said Caro. Was she being

impolite? She was a bit, but getting names right was important, everybody knew that.

'Caroline,' continued Gam, ignoring the interruption, 'we do *not* wolf our food down in this house. I daresay you are hungry and perhaps you've had a long day, but at this present moment, you really do rather resemble a stone-age cave dweller.'

Caro laughed. It was partly a nervous laugh and partly a real one, because comparing her to a stone-age cave dweller was actually quite funny. She had certainly never been compared to one before.

Gam laid her knife and fork down and stared at her hard.

'Tell me, is your mother still gallivanting all over the world?'

'If you mean, is she in great demand for her whistling skills, then yes!' said Caro truthfully.

'She whistles?' said Albie, his head shooting up.

'Albie,' rapped out Great Aunt Mary brusquely. 'Do not speak with your mouth full.'

'She's whistled in *all* the best places,' said Caro, who was proud of her mother and never tired of telling people how amazing she was. 'Prussia, Borneo, all the way up the Amazon.'

Jacinta had been invited *back* to the Amazon, to

perform at the Manaus Opera House. That's where she should have been coming home from yesterday, but instead she'd... Caro pushed the thought away.

'Just wait till you hear her!' she boasted. 'Have you ever heard Mozart's "Queen of the Night"?'

Albie shook his head.

Or Bach's "Badinerie"?'

No.

'Well anyway, she can whistle them note perfect.'

'Hmmph!' tutted Gam.

'Women,' said Caro, unstoppable now, 'have been whistling professionally since before the First World War. It's an undervalued art form.' That's what her mum said, anyway. 'They're called *siffleuses*. People say when you see my mum whistling, you can't help but smile.'

Albie stared at Caro in a sort of wonderment.

'I'd like to hear that,' he said quietly.

'Yes, yes,' said Gam irritably, clearly unimpressed. 'That's quite enough about whistling for today thank you very much. What of your father?'

'I don't have one,' said Caro. She was surprised Gam didn't know even this most basic piece of information. She mustn't have talked to mum in aeons.

'*Everybody*,' said Gam, 'has a father.'

Carefully, Caro carved a line down the middle of her shepherd's pie. The knife made a scraping noise on the plate which was very fine bone china.

'Mum was young,' said Caro. 'They were …' She searched for the right word. 'Incompatible.' ('Good riddance,' was what Jacinta had actually said.) 'He went away.' ('Thank goodness.') 'And anyway, two mums suits me fine.'

Gam snorted and a piece of shepherd's pie shot out of her nose. For the first time, Albie caught Caro's eye and she detected a hint of a smile.

'I've never heard of anything so preposterous. Two mothers? That… *publican* woman? The one who rang to say you had to come here? As I expected, you are a wild little thing just like your mother.'

'That's rude, that is!' said Caro. Ronnie had said to be polite, to not cause trouble. But surely if she could hear what Gam was saying she'd change her mind?

Caro opened her mouth to deliver a few more home truths, but Gam was still talking, and it was as if Caro hadn't even spoken and Gam was a train gathering steam.

'Your hair, your manners, the way you eat. It's all quite deplorable. If you are going to live in this house, you will have to change your ways. I failed your mother, but I *will* tame you.'

'You can't *tame* anyone,' said Caro, unable to contain herself any longer, flinging down her fork so forcefully it skidded across the table and crashed into Albie's plate. 'I don't *want* to be here, I've come under ... duress. As soon as I can, I'll leave.'

'How dare you!' said Gam. She picked up her napkin and dabbed at her mouth indignantly. 'You can eat the rest of your supper in your bedroom. I do not want to see or hear from you until breakfast.'

'Don't worry, I'm going,' said Caro, pushing her chair back with such a clatter that Gam put her hands over her ears. Then, grabbing her plate of half-finished shepherd's pie she stalked angrily out, all thoughts of being polite quite thoroughly extinguished.

* * *

Upstairs, Caro flung herself onto her bed and sobbed into her pillow at the unfairness of it all. How was she going to be able to bear it? How could she spend any more time in the company of that horrid woman downstairs? A woman who was so rude and dismissive of her two mothers, who she loved most in the world? She felt sick. Sick for home and Ronnie and Waterloo. She couldn't *wait* until tomorrow, when she would get out of this heartless place and travel back on the tube to see Horace. The thought made her feel calmer. Hang on in there, she told herself. *Courage*. She wiped away her tears and tried to eat the remains of the shepherd's pie, but it had gone stone cold and she wasn't hungry anyway.

She wanted to go outside now and get His Nibs. But what if Gam saw her? What would she do if she saw the rabbit? Judging by what Caro had seen so far, she would probably shoot him and turn him into a pie!

After some time, she heard Albie come upstairs and tap on her door.

'Caro!' he whispered.

What did he want? Did he want to make friends after all? She didn't answer. She was too tired to talk. She heard his steps recede and then a thumping sound coming from the room next door – presumably his bedroom. *Thump thump thump*. She wondered what on earth he was doing. But she was still too angry and upset to go and see. Gradually, the sky outside darkened. In the garden, the pools of light reflected from the house's windows clicked off one by one.

After a while she could no longer hear Marks padding about upstairs.

She was desperate to snatch up His Nibs and bury her face in his fur. But good sense told her she must wait until everyone was asleep. Then she would climb down there and rescue him, and smuggle him into her room.

Caro dragged the suitcase out from under the bed and retrieved the bird painting. She thought it probably *was* her mother's because it was beautiful and Jacinta loved beautiful things. A tear squeezed out of her eye and wended its way down her cheek. She would give *anything* to hear her mum whistling 'The Flower Duet' now. It was the tune she always whistled when she was coming home.

Carefully, Caro tucked the painting underneath her pillow and then lay with her head on top of it. If this *had* been Jacinta's bedroom when she'd been a girl, then had *she* stomped up the stairs after rows with Gam? The thought was quietly comforting and, along with the proximity to the painting, made Caro feel not quite so alone.

Outside, a car puttered its way up East Heath Road and in the distance a siren wailed. Apart from that, it was deadly quiet, like being in the middle of the countryside. Caro missed the creaks and groans of the pub, the trains rumbling past, the bell calling last orders, and the sound of the regulars tumbling out onto the street at closing time. A tiny part of her even missed Toby. In fact, if she could somehow be magicked home right now, she would be nice to Toby for the rest of her life.

Downstairs, the grandfather clock struck eleven.

Surely Gam, who seemed as old as a dinosaur, would be safely asleep by now? His Nibs would be wondering where she had got to. And what if there were foxes? She needed to get outside now, and quick.

It was no good climbing out of her window. Her room was at the front of the house, and she remembered glancing up at the red-brick façade just before she had pushed the pram into the bush. It had been flat-fronted. She couldn't remember seeing a single foothold. Not ideal for climbing then.

But the back of the house, would that do instead? If she could climb down that way, there was bound to be a side passage leading to the front.

Quiet as a mouse, Caro left her room and felt her way along the third-floor landing. The hallway was dark and shadowy and would've been pitch black if it hadn't been for a helpful shaft of moonlight slanting in through the large window. At Albie's bedroom door she paused. She could still hear a thudding sound coming from inside, like someone doing gymnastics in socked feet. A part of her wanted to turn the door handle, catch him at whatever he was up to, but more pressing was to get His Nibs.

In the nursery, she heaved the sash window open. It groaned tiredly, as though it hadn't been shifted in an age. She stuck her head out and saw it was a short drop to a flat area below, which was actually the roof of the second-floor bay window.

Carefully, she slid over the window ledge. The flat area was hemmed in by an iron railing. And now she could see a drainpipe to the right, running down the side of the house.

Caro felt a quiver of excitement. She wasn't frightened. This was by far the best thing she'd done all day. Good job she hadn't put her slippers on. She needed her bare feet as much as her hands to cling and grasp and to find the right holds. Climbing over the railing, she made the short leap to the drainpipe, wrapped her legs and arms around it, and scuttled down until she came to a pitched roof. That was easy to slide down, bump, bump, bump, and here was a wooden strut – perfect! She reached for it and shinned down until she found herself on a large balcony stretching across the width of the house.

Big glass doors glittered in the black night air. Might that be Gam's bedroom? Caro could just picture her lying propped up on several pillows, her black cap still in place and her umbrella by her side. Mustn't hang about here too long. She peered over the wooden railing – and bingo! – there was a pillar, one of four, reaching up to support the balcony. All she had to do was slide down, and ... there.

She was in the garden.

The lawn looked ghostly in the moonlight; the grass felt wet on the soles of her feet. Quickly she padded round the side of the house to the front and – yes! – there was the bush.

She pushed her way into it, denser than she remembered, dark leaves brushing against her hair and her face, twigs cracking underfoot. All she wanted now was to gather up her precious rabbit, to feel his weight in her arms, his warm little quivers and the steady beat of his heart.

'There, there, my darling,' she muttered.

The silver wheels of the pram gleamed. She felt for the hood and pushed it back, plunging her arms inside.

But there was nothing.

The pram was empty.
No hay. No carrot tops. No cauliflower leaves.
No warm, quivering rabbit.
His Nibs had gone.

Chapter Five

It was as if her heart had stopped beating.

What if a fox *had* got him? Or what if he'd gone looking for her and got lost?

But logic told her he couldn't carry his own food. Or his bedding.

In a panic, she crashed about in the bush.

'His Nibs,' she whispered frantically. 'Where are you?'

Onto the gravel drive, searching for a flash of white and two splodges of ginger. Back into the bushes, down on her hands and knees, crawling into the densest, darkest parts.

Nothing.

Out into the open again, running back and forth, like a crazed animal, eyes wide, skirting the perimeter of the garden, calling out in a hoarse whisper.

Onto the street, panic coming in great uncontrollable waves. Looking up, down, across to the heath.

Why had she abandoned him? She should've just taken him into the house with her in the first place; who cared what Gam thought? All that time she'd wasted unpacking and eating silly shepherd's pie and now...

Had he been *stolen*?

Caro buried her face in her hands. She couldn't bear it. She would give anything to hear the *thud thud* of his rabbit feet, to see him bounding towards her, his little eyes winking and blinking because it had all just been a game of hide and seek.

Her mind stopped racing for a minute. Focused on the words she had just thought.

Thud thud.

Where had she heard that?

In a flash she ran back around the side of the house, across the lawn, and flung herself up, grabbing hold of the balcony, hauling herself over like a spider, arms and legs confident now, knowing where the footholds were, where the places to grab on to were.

On she scuttled, anger blooming. How dare that boy lay his hands on her rabbit? She'd guessed he was a snoop!

Furiously she scrabbled across the pitched roof (much harder going up than sliding down) hauled herself up the drainpipe, climbed over the railings and slithered in through the window.

It took a matter of seconds to cross the nursery floor, fling herself onto the landing and burst into Albie's room.

A figure lay hunched up, fast asleep and gently snoring. At the foot of the bed crouched His Nibs, quietly working his way through a mound of cabbage leaves. Caro felt a burst of relief as he glanced up mid chew. His little black eyes blinked at her, completely oblivious to the panic he had just caused.

Caro strode across the floor and shook Albie roughly by the shoulder.

'How dare you!' she hissed, flicking on the lamp that sat on Albie's bedside table.

Albie grunted and struggled awake. He stared at her in confusion.

'You stole my rabbit!' she said to enlighten him.

'What?' he muttered and rubbed his eyes. 'I didn't steal him, I was just keeping him safe.'

'He didn't need keeping safe!'

Albie sat up. His hair was sticking out all over the place. His red-and-white-striped pyjamas were at least three sizes too big for him.

'*You* abandoned him,' he protested. 'I saw you hide him in the bushes, and then you just came inside and left him out there!'

'So you *were* snooping!'

'I wasn't!' said Albie.

Caro felt like shaking him. How could he not see that what he had done was just plain wrong? She stepped back and a knitting needle stabbed her in the foot. There were tons of them scattered all over the floor.

'For goodness' sake,' she said, sweeping them up and chucking them into a pile in the corner of the room.

'Careful!' said Albie.

'Look,' she said, sitting down on the bed and trying as hard as she could to be patient. 'I was only hiding him because Ronnie said I wasn't allowed to bring him here...'

'Well, Ronnie was right. Mrs Monday hates all animals.'

'She can't hate *all* animals.'

Albie gave her a look that said she didn't know what

she was talking about.

'I wasn't allowed to bring my guinea pigs *or* my gerbils when I came,' he sniffed. 'She made me give them back to the pet shop.'

Give them back to the pet shop? That must have been awful. But ... if Albie knew that ...

'How could you have fetched him inside then?' Caro demanded. 'If you know she hates animals so much? What if she'd caught you ... what if she catches us now?'

'But he can't stay outside in the pram all night! What about the foxes?' Albie retorted. 'What if he ran away?'

'He wouldn't,' said Caro stubbornly.

'I tried to tell you, I knocked on your door ... but you ignored me.'

Caro stood up. Her heart was still hammering.

'You should be saying sorry to me, bursting in like that, frightening me awake!' said Albie.

'Are you crazy?' she said. 'Just mind your own business in future and leave me to look after my own rabbit.'

As soon as the words were out, Caro felt a pang of guilt. He was an orphan. He had to live with Gam *all the time.* Giving up his guinea pigs and gerbils couldn't have been easy. She imagined what she would feel like if Gam made her send His Nibs back to a pet shop.

The red-hot anger, which had consumed her a moment earlier, slipped away.

'Promise not to tell?' she said, crouching down to scoop up His Nibs. He lay in her arms all warm and heavy, his fur sweetly comforting.

''Course I won't,' Albie said. 'I'm not your enemy, you know.' And with a last, reproachful look, he flumped back down and pulled the covers over his head.

* * *

The next morning, Caro woke early. If Gam hated animals as much as Albie said she did, then she would *have* to keep His Nibs a secret. She couldn't risk him being sent to a pet shop like Albie's guinea pigs and gerbils. She turned over and draped an arm around him. He snuffled happily and twitched his lovely ears. She imagined there was an invisible piece of elastic connecting the pair of them. What would happen if the elastic stretched and stretched and then – snap!

'I'll never let that happen, never!' she said. For now, he would have to stay hidden in her bedroom. Even though he was used to racing about all over the place; even though he loved nothing more than to bound and jump.

But it would be OK. She was going to go to Waterloo every day, and she would smuggle him out with her.

Now His Nibs hopped off the bed and stood expectantly by the door. Caro glanced at her watch. Only six-thirty. His nose twitched as though he was saying, 'Come on, Caro. Get out of our bed!' The house was quiet, everyone still asleep. It was probably safe to take him across the road to the heath, where there was all that grass waiting to be munched and they could hunt for dandelion leaves.

Just for a short while.

Downstairs, in a cupboard in the hall, amongst the hats and scarves and wellington boots, Caro found a very large, grey coat.

'Wait a sec,' she whispered to His Nibs as she shrugged it on. The sleeves were so long, the cuffs covered her hands and the hem trailed on the floor.

'Ready,' she said, and she hefted the rabbit up and arranged him so that he was hidden inside the folds of billowing fabric. Then she hurried outside.

It was a glorious day. On the other side of the road, the sun rippled across the endless heath; the sky blazed a deep blue, and blossom fought its way out of the buds on the trees.

But Caro had barely reached the gate when the front door opened behind her.

'Caroline Monday, where on earth do you think you are going?'

Caro's heart sank as she slowly turned around. It was Gam, fully dressed in her droopy black, her green umbrella by her side.

'Did I *give* you permission to leave the house?'

'No, but ...' Had Gam being lying in wait for her? She must have really good ears. Snuggled inside the coat, His Nibs shifted position. Any minute now he'd probably burst out and give Gam a heart attack. Surreptitiously, Caro tightened her hold on him.

Gam's eyes swept over Caro and then narrowed suspiciously. Could she tell? Surely not. The coat was huge, the billowing folds giving nothing away.

'That's not your coat, is it? Are you in the habit of taking property that doesn't belong to you? Take it off at once and come back inside.'

The words were rapped out, cold and business-like. Caro hesitated. She didn't know what to do.

'Caroline Monday, did you hear what I just said?'

Caro took a step towards Gam. She couldn't take

the coat off! Gam would come face to face with His Nibs!

'I'm terribly cold,' she tried.

'I *said*, take it off,' the elderly lady snapped and her nostrils flared angrily. 'It's not yours.'

Caro sighed.

Reluctantly she slipped one arm out of the coat and...

At the same time, a high-pitched scream came from inside the house.

In an instant, Gam whipped round and hurried back inside; Caro rushed into the bush, deposited His Nibs inside the pram and then hurtled back into the house two steps behind Gam.

Albie was sitting at the bottom of the stairs clutching his ankle.

'I slipped!' he said.

'You silly boy!' said Gam unsympathetically, while Caro shoved the coat back into the cupboard. 'Can you stand on it?'

Albie got up gingerly and walked a few steps. 'Yes.'

'Good. Caroline stop gawping. Come and wash your hands both of you – breakfast won't eat itself.'

* * *

'I'm willing to overlook,' said Gam when they were sitting around the table, 'yesterday's little tantrum. I shall put it down to first-day nerves.'

Caro's mouth was full of cornflakes. More cardboardy and stale-tasting than the ones at home. She wasn't going to apologise for her behaviour yesterday, so she concentrated on chewing instead. All she had to do was get through breakfast, and then she and His Nibs would make another attempt at escape and stay out for the whole day.

'There are rules that must be abided by,' continued Gam as she poured the tea, holding the pot quite high so it fell in a noisy stream into her cup. 'The most important one being that you may never go out on your own. I don't know *where* you were setting off to this morning, Caroline, but any more escapades like that will *not* be tolerated. An hour in the company of Marks – until the new nanny arrives – is all I will allow. You can let off steam on the heath and if you're very lucky she might take you to the sweet shop afterwards, isn't that right, Albie?'

Albie nodded mutely.

Caro nearly spat out her cornflakes. An hour a day? In Waterloo she was allowed out at all hours. Come the holidays, she'd cut doorstep-size slices of bread for cheese sandwiches, and then she and Horace would just disappear for *ages*. Sometimes they stayed in the Rubbles. Other times they caught a bus and went all over London. They'd been to Hyde Park and Oxford Street, the big museums in South Kensington, and all the way along the canal from Little Venice to Islington.

One hour!

And not even on her own.

'But I came here alone. On the tube! If I can do that, surely...'

'You came here on your own because this "other" mother of yours allowed it. Now you are in *my* care, you follow my rules. And that is all there is to it.' Gam pursed her lips and began what Ronnie would call 'a performance' of spreading marmalade on her toast. Taking far too long over it and with unnecessary flourishes. She was rather a dramatic person, Caro thought.

Caro stared down at her own plate of toast and marmalade. If she was only allowed out for one hour a day – with Marks – how on earth was she going to get to Waterloo?

'You really have chosen the most *inconvenient* time to visit, Caroline,' Gam went on. 'Because we are between nannies it means poor Marks is saddled with you both. It's not her job and...'

A visit! Caro would hardly describe it as that. A visit sounded pleasant, whereas this enforced stay was quite the opposite.

'Not to worry, Mary,' said Marks soothingly. She had appeared to clear the table. 'I'm sure young Caro will abide by your rules and stay out of trouble, isn't that right, Caro?' She blew her fringe out of her eyes and met Caro's gaze.

All Caro could do was nod back glumly. She thought about His Nibs waiting in the pram buried in the bushes, Horace waiting in the Rubbles, wondering where she was. The gym waiting to be built. And the precious weeks ticking by and no practising being done.

This was going to be harder than her worst imaginings. She wasn't sure if she would be able to manage it. But for Ronnie's sake, she must at least try.

* * *

'Is it true?' Caro asked Albie later. They'd been sent up to the nursery after breakfast and told to occupy themselves until Marks was ready to take them outside for the allotted hour. Albie was making some sort of house thing with the knitting needles. It was two storeys high and had different levels which were connected by a ramp.

'What?' he mumbled. His breathing was really loud when he was concentrating.

'That you're only allowed out with an adult? For one hour a day?'

'Yep,' said Albie. He wasn't really listening to her. He was trying to saw one of the knitting needles in half with a penknife.

'It's all ruined then!' said Caro.

Albie stopped fiddling with the penknife and looked up. 'What is?

'How can I make my gym if I can't get back to the Rubbles and see Horace?'

'What's the Rubbles?' he said. 'And who's Horace?'

Because there was no one else to talk to, and even though he was only a kid, Caro explained how Horace was her best friend; how she never went a day without talking to him; and how she only had fifty-two weeks to practise her gymnastics or else she wouldn't be ready to unleash her talents on the world when she left school.

'You'll get used to it,' he said quietly. 'And Marks is OK when you get to know her ...'

She was about to snap back that she didn't want to get used to it, but she stopped herself just in time. Albie didn't even have a choice. He was stuck here for ever because...

A horrible thought rushed at her like a wave. What if Jacinta was dead like Albie's parents? What if *that* was why she and Ronnie had not heard from her? Maybe Ronnie really *did* think that was a possibility and that's why she had started saying all that stuff about families and who might look after Caro if...

Stop it! Stop it! Ronnie would say, 'Stick to the facts. Don't imagine things you don't know.'

'Albie! Caro!' shouted Marks from downstairs, interrupting Caro's thoughts. 'Time to go. You ready?'

It was ten o'clock. In Waterloo, Horace would be waiting for her. She could try to phone him. But the Braithwaites didn't have a telephone. And if he was in the Rubbles, he wouldn't hear the phone ringing in the telephone box at the end of his street.

How else could she let him know what was going on?

'Have you got a stamp?' she asked Albie. 'And an envelope?'

'No,' he said, looking scared. 'But I know where Mrs Monday keeps them. I can get them for you if you like.'

'Yes please,' she said. 'Quickly!'

While he was gone, she found a piece of paper and scrawled:

> She won't let me come back!
> No gym this summer.

When Albie reappeared he watched as she shoved the note inside the envelope, addressed it and stamped it. She could tell he had a thousand questions but was too shy to ask them.

'Is there a post box nearby?' she asked.

'By the sweet shop,' he said. 'I'll show you.'

'Thanks,' said Caro, relieved that he was being helpful.

'Well, do you want to go or not?' yelled Marks from downstairs.

'Coming!'

* * *

The next few days were a struggle.

On the plus side there were plenty of climbing opportunities inside the house: three flights of stairs for Caro to walk up and down on her hands; banisters to use as a balancing beam; doorways to jump up to and swing from.

But it was not the same as the promised gym. Caro's limbs still longed to be challenged, to stretch and leap. She missed testing her body's limits – the tantalising sense of fear laced with exhilaration. And Gam seemed to have a miraculous ability to appear whenever she was practising. Typically, she would emerge from wherever she had been hiding, brandishing her umbrella.

'Get down, Caroline! Stop that right now! Do you think I've got time to take you to accident and emergency? Go to your room and stay there until I say otherwise!'

Albie seemed adept at keeping his head down and staying out of Gam's way, but Caro couldn't seem to do anything right. She wasn't quiet enough; she didn't brush her hair properly; she mustn't kneel at the table.

It was always 'don't do this, don't do that'.

'If you'd just let me out,' said Caro practically, 'the house would be quiet and there'd be no one to get on your nerves.' That wasn't causing trouble. It was being helpful. It was offering solutions to problems.

But Gam silenced Caro's suggestions with a look shot through with daggers. She sent her to collect knitting needles and wool from Albie. Then she presented her with a book called *How to Knit*.

'I shall expect to see a scarf later this afternoon,' she said briskly.

But Caro couldn't sit still for long enough to learn how to slide the stitches from one needle to the other, and the wool got into a terrible knotty tangle and anyway, she preferred unravelling it, laying it in a long line on the floor and then pretending it was a tightrope. Of course, Gam caught her at it when she suddenly appeared at the nursery door to inspect Caro's progress. Luckily, His Nibs was hiding behind the door.

'Go to your room!' barked Gam.

When she was finally allowed back downstairs, Gam sat Caro at the piano. She showed her which keys her fingers should rest on and set her to learn 'Three Blind Mice'. But Caro already knew a tune: it was called 'Chopsticks' – Horace's Aunty Sandra had taught her. She bashed it out with any old fingers, it was lively and loud and much better than boring old 'Three Blind Mice'. Gam flinched dramatically, as if the notes that Caro played were flying knives, and sent her back to her room *again*.

The only reason Caro didn't mind being endlessly sent to her room was because that was where His Nibs was hiding.

Keeping him hidden was difficult. Gam never

seemed to go out, and when she did, she came back suddenly and unexpectedly. It was far from ideal. But in the evening when Gam was in the lounge watching one of her programmes, and Marks was upstairs painting and listening to records on her gramophone, Caro made Albie keep lookout near the lounge door while the rabbit bounded up and down the upstairs hallway. Once, she'd opened the nursery window, draped His Nibs around her shoulders and started to climb outside. But Albie had got tearful. It hadn't been clear if he was more worried about Gam coming out of her lair and finding Caro gone, or if he was scared that Caro might leave and never come back.

Wherever she went, Albie trailed after her with his knitting needles and wool. He really was the most timid creature she had ever met. She learned that he had been with Gam for two years; that he still missed his parents (she could hear him whimpering himself to sleep through the walls); and that he was lonely. The house thing that he had been constructing, made out of size-thirteen knitting needles and pink wool, turned out to be a sort of makeshift hutch. It was an ingenious contraption, on two levels and with connecting ramps.

It was kind of him to have made it, and Caro was genuinely thankful. But, he was no replacement for

Horace. First, he was too young. And second, he had been living in Gam's world and following her inexplicable rules for so long that he didn't seem to have the slightest idea about freedom or what he was missing.

On top of that, because he was a genuine orphan, she couldn't even share her worries with him about her own family. She knew it wouldn't be fair to burden him with her anxieties about Jacinta's whereabouts and Ronnie's absence. Not when he was still mourning his own parents.

Ronnie, who phoned every day, said not to worry.

'Jacinta will be fine. No news is good news,' she said.

'When are you coming home?' asked Caro.

'As soon as I can, Caro.' Ronnie didn't sound like herself. She sounded tired.

'You're being good, aren't you?'

'Of course I am,' said Caro. She wanted to say, 'I hate it here, I miss you and I miss Mum and I can't bear it much longer.'

But instead, she remembered Ronnie's anxious face and her droopy eyes. If only Marjorie's husband, Harry, would hurry up and come back from wherever he was at sea.

And how she longed for Horace, and chatting

nineteen to the dozen about everything and anything; Horace, who always understood her worries straight away, without even very much explanation.

The allotted hour outside wasn't much fun either. Especially with His Nibs still stuck inside.

All Marks wanted to do was get on with her art. 'This isn't part of my job description,' she would mutter as they waded through the long grass of the heath towards the ponds.

When she wasn't looking, Albie and Caro would stuff their pockets full of dandelion leaves and on the way home they'd stop at the sweet shop, which Marks seemed to think made up for everything.

But even though Caro loved a bag of bullseyes and liquorice shoelaces as much as the next person, it didn't make up for anything. She was at her wits' end. Until the third day, when Horace arrived.

* * *

It was the afternoon, after lunch, and Albie and Caro had been sent to the nursery and told to be quiet while Gam had a nap. Marks had gone to meet a friend in a coffee bar. Albie was inventing a knitting-needle ladder, with really thick wool which he had plaited into strong rope. Caro had walked round the perimeter of the room ten times on her hands. Now she was lying on her back drumming her heels on the floor and trying (unsuccessfully) to whistle.

A tapping noise at the window caught her attention, and then another and another. Someone was throwing gravel at the glass.

Jumping up, Caro dashed over to the window and leaned out. Her heart did a giant leap. It was Horace! Standing by the gate and waving. He was looking ever so Horace-y, dressed like a beatnik in a huge jumper, and with a French beret on his head.

Even better, he was clutching Jacinta's bag of tools!

She waved 'hello' frantically. He'd got her letter! He'd come!

Caro turned and strode past Albie towards the door. Gam was asleep. Marks was out at her coffee bar. Surely she could escape for a couple of hours?

'I'm going out,' she said to Albie.

'What?' he looked up, confusion spreading across his features.

'If anyone comes looking,' she commanded, 'say I'm in my room with a terrible headache and that I mustn't be disturbed.'

Albie looked aghast. 'You mean, lie? Why, Caro?

She won't fall for it! Please don't go out! She'll go bananas...'

Caro, who was already halfway out of the door, stopped.

'Oh, Albie!'

His eyes were filling with tears. Why couldn't he be a bit braver? Too late Caro realised she should have been paying him more attention, teaching him to stand up for himself. He needed to be a bit more ... what was that word? Robust.

She came back into the room and knelt down beside him, gripping him by the shoulders in what she hoped was a reassuring manner. She tried to will brave thoughts from her own mind into his.

'I won't be long, honest, Albie. Stick to the story. Please.'

She ran into her bedroom and scooped up His Nibs. Back in the nursery, determinedly ignoring Albie's agonised expression, she arranged the rabbit around her shoulders, climbed out of the window and began her descent.

'At last!' said Horace as she tiptoed across the gravel. It crunched noisily, like a giant attacking a bowl of Rice Krispies. She hoped Gam was in a really, really deep sleep.

'You brought the tools!' said Caro, It was so great to see him again.

Horace grinned back at her. 'I thought, if you can't come to me, I'll come to you. We can build the gym over there. There's masses of space.' He nodded in the direction of the heath. 'Hello stranger,' he said to His Nibs, and the rabbit bobbed his head in greeting.

'We'll have to be quick,' said Caro. 'If she catches us ...' She mimed being stabbed by a dagger, and Horace giggled and then did his own mime, collapsing to the floor, twisting and turning in a show of agony and suffering great death throes.

'Honestly, Horace,' said Caro, now almost helpless with laughter, 'I'm not lying! She's a dragon!'

'Caro!' a whisper came from behind her.

Caro whipped around. It wasn't Gam. It wasn't Marks. It was Albie. Looking scared witless.

'Is he all right?' He was staring at Horace who was still playing dead on the floor.

'Of course he's all right. What are you doing?' she said furiously, grabbing him and dragging him outside the gate so that they couldn't be seen from the house.

'I want to come, too,' he said. His eyes darted pleadingly from Caro to Horace, who was now busily dusting off his trousers.

'Well you can't! Go back inside now!' said Caro. Any minute Gam would wake up and hear them. What if Albie started to cry and make a fuss? She lowered her voice to a whisper, trying to sound kind, cajoling. 'You need to be there in case she comes upstairs. We agreed!'

'We didn't,' said Albie. 'You said it, but I never ...'

For the first time ever, Albie looked mutinous. He raised his chin defiantly and held her eye.

Inwardly Caro sighed. He couldn't come. He wasn't brave enough. He'd ruin everything.

'You're too frightened to come. You don't want to, really.' Caro reached out a hand to grasp his shoulder again, intending to give him a comforting squeeze, but he shook her off.

'I *do* want to!'

'Caro ...' started Horace.

'I saved you,' Albie piped up. 'Accidentally on purpose.'

'What are you talking about?'

'When Mrs Monday was telling you to take off that coat, and I'd already *told* you she hates animals. If she'd seen His Nibs, she would've sent him away and what would you have done then?'

Slowly realisation dawned.

'You mean you pretended to fall down the stairs for me?' she said.

'Yes,' he said.

'Impressive!' said Horace, and Albie smiled properly now. A smile of pride.

'I know you want to make your gym,' he said, quickly now. 'And if you let me come, I can show you the perfect place on the heath. Where my parents used to take me before...'

'Let the kid come, Caro,' said Horace. He was always trying to include people. At school he was the one who spotted the lost souls and suggested that he and Caro look after them. He was kind like that.

Albie cast a grateful look at Horace. Caro didn't think he had ever looked at *her* like that. It made her feel bad.

'Come on then,' she said. 'Show us this place.'

* * *

Albie took them to a part of the heath he called 'the Wilds'; all untamed with grass growing tall like prairie grass, odd stumps of trees and thickety bushes running rampant. It was almost as good as the Rubbles.

'This is perfect Caro, isn't it?' said Horace, clapping Albie on the back.

It *was* perfect. There was a tree that had half blown

down and branches of different sizes lay scattered about. Opposite was a short thick stump with a branch sticking out at right angles that was several feet off the ground. If they could find some other similar-sized branches to attach between the stump and the half blown-down tree, they could fashion a rudimentary balancing beam, which – hopefully – would stretch between the two.

'Thank you, Albie,' said Caro gratefully. She knew that she and Horace would never have found this place on their own. Not without weeks and weeks of searching. Hampstead Heath was huge.

Together, they unpacked the bag of tools and spread them out on the ground: the saw, the hammer, the jars of nails. Then they started hunting for the right-sized branches.

A solid-looking branch, just the right thickness, lay a short way from where Caro was standing. She reached down to grab it. And–

Did it just twitch?

Caro took a step closer.

It wasn't a branch at all. It was a leg, clad in brown woollen trousers.

Lying almost hidden in the grass was the gentleman she had met on the bench near the tube station! He was fast asleep, his head resting on a newspaper pillow.

Caro coughed, and the man slowly opened one eye, then two. The first thing he saw was His Nibs, who had hopped over behind Caro.

'Ginger?' he said, sitting up abruptly. 'No, it can't be Ginger, of course it's not.' He rubbed his eyes with large, gnarled hands. His thumbs were almost the size of the sausage rolls that Ronnie served up in the pub at lunchtime.

'Victor!' said Caro. 'Hello! We met on that bench near the station. Remember? You picked some chickweed for His Nibs.'

The rabbit's nose twitched in greeting.

'Well I never,' said the gentleman. 'You were having a hard day. If I remember rightly, I wished you *cou-rage*. Things a bit better now?'

'Much better,' said Caro. Because it truly did feel like that at this moment in time – away from the house, out in the open, with Horace and with the tools and with their gym-building plans alive and well again.

Victor stretched, and Caro heard odd clanking sounds coming from inside his coat.

'Oh! There's more than one of you!' he said.

Caro turned to see Albie and Horace approaching cautiously.

'It's all right,' she said. 'We know each other.'

Victor had been kind to her. And besides, she was used to all sorts in the pub. Ronnie always said she was a good judge of character. She could tell that the gentleman was not out to cause trouble. She nodded at Horace. He nodded back.

'Victor, this is Horace and this is Albie.'

'Greetings,' said Victor. And he reached inside his coat and drew out an impressive-looking gold watch on a chain. 'That time already! No wonder I'm half-starved. Anyone for tea?'

'Yes please!' said Albie.

They watched as Victor built a little fire out of sticks, and when the flames started to leap about enthusiastically, he set some water to boil in an old tin can. He was a 'gentleman of the road', he said.

'D'you mean a tramp?' asked Albie.

Albie seemed different, thought Caro. A liveliness had crept across his quiet features. A curiosity. It hadn't done him any good to be shut up for so long.

'That's a good way of describing it. I do a lot of tramping, up and down the highways and byways, bedding down here, there and everywhere. I have no *fixed* abode.'

He stopped talking as he concentrated on spooning tea leaves into an enamelled teapot.

'Last month I woke up in a ditch – a very nice ditch it was too: sheltered, mossy, sweet-smelling, under the pines, a carpet of rosemary – and I just knew, felt it in my bones, some would say, that it was time to come back... I come back from time to time, you see to—'

'Are *all* your belongings in there?' interrupted Albie, staring in open admiration at the sack on the end of the stick.

'Everything I own is in that pack, or on my back.' Victor opened his coat to display a neat row of ribbon loops, hanging from which were all manner of things: cutlery, a small pair of scissors, a hand mirror, a comb, a pair of spectacles, and a tin cup. 'A gentleman doesn't need a wealth of possessions for a wealthy life, you know.'

'Did you sew all those in yourself, sir?' Horace leaned in to get a better look. He was especially interested in the stitching on the ribbon loops.

'I did,' said Victor. 'Not much you can't do with a needle and thread.'

Horace agreed, and Caro struck a pose and showed Victor the cape that Horace had made her, and Victor admired it and told Horace he would go far.

'We're trying to make something too,' said Caro, indicating the half fallen-down tree. 'A balancing beam so I can practise my gymnastics.'

Victor appraised the tree. 'Well, I'd say you've picked a good one there. Shouldn't be too hard to fix up, and I see you've got a nice set of tools.'

Any other adult (apart from Caro's mum, Jacinta) would have said, 'You can't possibly build that on your own,' and given them a lecture about tools being dangerous, and children not being allowed to handle hammers and saws. But not Victor. He was nice. A trusting sort.

'Excuse me, Victor, could I have this, please?' Horace was waving about the newspaper that Victor had been using as a pillow. He unfolded it, smoothing out the pages so that they could see what had caught his interest.

> Lady Dockitt distraught. Back from latest cruise to find Old Master stolen. Believed to be the work of an elusive gang known as the Snakes, say Scotland Yard.

'Why are you collecting stuff about the Snakes?' asked Caro in surprise. She knew Horace had a scrapbook full of photographs and postcards that he called his 'inspiration'. But this was hardly that.

'It's the dress!' said Horace, pointing at a photograph showing a woman stepping out of a sleek sports car.

'It looks like she's got it on upside down,' giggled Albie.

He was right, Caro thought. The dress in the picture was like an upside-down flowerpot, wide at the top and narrow at the bottom.

'It's not funny!' protested Horace. 'It's tremendous. She's wearing the party dress that Yves made especially for her to wear to the spring ball in Paris!'

'Yves Saint Laurent,' explained Caro to Victor. 'Horace's hero. He's obsessed.'

'He works for the house of Dior,' said Horace, ignoring Caro. 'I *admire* him a great deal.'

'Of course you may have it, Horace,' said Victor graciously. 'Now, tea.' And he dug about in his pockets and brought out several interesting-looking packages wrapped in greaseproof paper. 'Fruit cake, scones, cucumber sandwiches anyone? If you are hungry?'

'Starving!' said Albie, eyes shining. 'I think this is the best day I've ever had! Since ... you know.'

So Victor poured the tea (besides the tin cup inside his coat, he had three more tucked away in his pack) and they shared out the edibles, and settled back against the various tree stumps, and quite forgot about the time, and the trouble they might be causing back at Heath View, as they listened to his stories about life on the road.

He'd slept in caves and treehouses and ramshackle barns; seen giant waterfalls and huge standing stones; and walked up roads that wound their way into mountains so high they disappeared into the clouds. He told them about the foxes he'd shared a den with when he was tired and cold and caught in a blizzard; and about the time his pack washed away down river, and just when he thought he would never see it again, it was rescued and returned by a stray dog.

'Albie?! Caro!'

Albie nearly choked on his third piece of fruit cake. Caro spurted out a mouthful of hot tea.

It was Marks, crashing her way through the long grass and now standing, hands on hips, looking down at them furiously. She blew her fringe out of her eyes like a dragon breathing fire. 'What on earth are you doing up here? I've been looking everywhere for you. There's been an intruder at the house. Mary's had to call the police! How could you have gone out? And who are they?' She glared at Horace and Victor. 'You'd better come back right now!'

Chapter Six

Caro's heart was pounding as she shoved the tools back inside the bag and hid it inside the hollow of the tree. Victor had taken off one of his many coats, and Caro said, 'Can I?' and without a question, Victor nodded 'yes', and Caro picked it up and put it on. Marks was already striding away, shouting over her shoulder at Caro and Albie to follow, so she didn't notice Caro scoop up His Nibs and hide him amongst the folds.

'Come back soon?' Caro gabbled to Horace. 'And thank you for the tea, Victor...'

'I said *come on*!' yelled Marks.

So they cut short their goodbyes and raced after her

across the heath, and Caro could sense Albie's terror and... was that a sob? She reached out and grabbed his hand and said, 'Don't worry, Albie. What's the worst Gam can do?'

'Keep us inside for ever?' he said.

They careened onto the gravel drive just as the policeman was leaving.

'Are you all right, Mary?' called Marks, running up the steps to Gam while Caro quickly darted into the bush, opened the voluminous coat, and deposited His Nibs in the pram.

'Where on earth were they?' asked Gam querulously. Her face was tight with worry. 'They had their hour out this morning! What's Caroline doing and what on earth is she wearing?'

'Well—' began Marks. But Gam didn't stop to listen.

'There *was* an intruder. I *heard* him creeping around upstairs.'

'But there's no sign of any break-in,' said the policeman patiently, as though he had already said it a thousand times before. 'I've been all over.'

Then, in an undertone to Marks who was nearest to him, 'Between you and me, the old lady might have been imagining it. What with all these stories circulating about the Snakes. Half of London thinks they're being targeted. We're getting called out all the time.'

'I heard that!' snapped Gam. 'I did *not* imagine it. It's you who's talking about the Snakes, whoever they are, not me. There was definitely *someone* upstairs.'

After the policeman had gone, they all trooped into the study and Gam gave them a long lecture of the 'you-are-only-allowed-out-once-a-day-and-if-you-can't-manage-that-you-won't-be-allowed-out-at-all' variety.

'I've a good mind to phone Mrs Rudd right now,' she said to Caro. '*You're* the ringleader. I'll tell her you've been leading young Albie astray. He was perfectly behaved before you came along.'

'It wasn't her fault,' said Albie bravely.

'No,' said Caro. 'It *was* my fault. I made Albie come...' She was still holding his hand and she felt him squeeze it gratefully. 'But please don't phone Ronnie. I promise I won't ever do it again.'

'I don't believe you for a minute,' said Gam tetchily. 'Thankfully, the new nanny is arriving tomorrow. Marks says she has found the perfect match.'

Marks gave a secret sort of smile. She looked particularly pleased with herself, Caro thought. Like a cat who had got the cream.

'So there will be an extra pair of eyes,' went on Gam,

'to keep you safe. And make certain you follow all the rules.'

* * *

That night, Caro tossed and turned. An extra pair of eyes to 'keep them safe'; to check they followed 'the rules'. The last thing she and Albie needed was a nanny person spying on them. How on earth would she manage to keep His Nibs a secret? Would the nanny insist on coming into her room?

And to make matters worse, why did it have to happen just as things had started to get better! What with Horace turning up and Albie showing them the Wilds, and the building of the gym under way.

Caro padded across the room and fetched His Nibs from his knitting-needle hutch. The moon slanted in through the window, making a stripe across the bed and up the wall. Caro peered at her watch. Already 2 a.m.! She made a nest for His Nibs next to her in bed, gently touched her mother's bird painting under the pillow, pictured herself in the beaten-up old car in the Rubbles, and, at last, drifted off.

The next time she opened her eyes, the moon had moved, its finger of light now stretching across the foot of the bed, pointing towards the door. She reached out for His Nibs, but he wasn't there.

Something was wrong.

There was a sound. A sort of scrabbling sound.

It's only His Nibs, she told herself. He makes all sorts of funny noises.

But what was that smell? It wasn't hay or cabbage leaves.

It was ... sharp. And sort of musty.

Like lemons ... and old leather.

Caro's gaze swivelled around the room's dark recesses. The chest of drawers. The bottom of the bed. The wardrobe ...

She opened her mouth to scream but nothing came out.

Something was lurking in the reflection of the mirror.

Something shadowy ... something human.

A robber!

A mad axeman!

Or a Snake!

Caro's mind raced, clutching at the possibilities, each one worse than the last.

It's not true. It's just your imagination, she told herself.

But ...

Had Gam been right? What if there *had* been an

intruder and now he was back, and he was looking for Caro?!

Caro snapped her eyes tight shut. *Pretend to be asleep. Play dead.*

She could hear the sound of her own blood pounding in her ears. And something else. Something scarier. The sound of another person breathing.

And on top of that, a rhythmic thumping.

Thump, thud, thump, thud, thump, thud.

Very slowly, Caro opened half an eye. Peered out from beneath her eyelashes.

The thumping sound was coming from His Nibs, caught in the strip of moonlight by the door, stamping his hind feet, his ears flat.

The thumping meant only one thing. It was what rabbits did when they sensed danger.

She *wasn't* imagining it. His Nibs knew too.

Caro jerked up, the paralysis broken, and now she did scream, and the thing in the mirror moved, crashing about, bashing into the wardrobe, and then blundering out of the door.

Caro leapt out of bed.

'Gam! Marks!' she yelled. 'There's someone in . . .'

She ran out onto the landing. But the person – the intruder – was already thundering down the stairs.

'What's going on?'

It was Gam, tottering out of her room in a pink dressing gown, blinking as the landing light flashed on.

'Mary, Caro!' Now Marks came flying down, her fringe sticking out at odd angles, clutching at a flower-splashed kimono; Albie sleepily opened his bedroom door.

Caro ignored them all, leaping down the stairs, taking two at a time, nearly slipping, and then she was on the ground floor, in the hall, and the front door was wide open and the cold night air flooded in.

Outside, the gravel drive was deserted.

Something nudged at her ankles.

His Nibs.

He'd followed her down.

'Caroline, what's happening?'

Gam was on the landing.

Quickly, Caro scooped up the rabbit, opened the door to the coat cupboard and popped him inside. She had just slammed it shut when Gam arrived at the foot of the stairs.

'You caught him!' she said proudly, looking from Caro to the coat cupboard.

'No,' said Caro.

Something about Gam's expression made her wish

she *had* caught him. For a strange, brief moment, she was aware that she wanted very much to please Gam, to make her proud.

But, 'I thought whoever it was might be hiding in there,' she explained, thinking quickly. 'They're not. They've gone.'

* * *

Gam telephoned the police again and they came in a car, screeching onto the drive with the siren on and the lights flashing.

'If you'd taken me seriously in the first place,' Gam snapped, 'then this wouldn't be happening and my great-niece wouldn't be frightened out of her wits.'

Caro glanced up, surprised. It was the first time she had heard Gam refer to her as her great-niece.

Marks had made cocoa and they were in the study, huddled round the gas fire in their dressing gowns. It was warm and cosy but Caro couldn't stop shaking. Albie held one of her hands and Marks held the other.

This time there were two policemen. One stood sentry by the door and the other sat with them, scribbling everything down in his notebook.

'Man or woman?' he asked.

Caro thought about the shadowy figure in the mirror and shivered.

'Man probably.' But she didn't know for sure.

'Accent?'

'He didn't *say* anything.'

Caro could see she wasn't providing the police with many clues. The only thing she could describe with any certainty was the smell.

And the fear.

She led the way to her bedroom and they all sniffed. There it was! Leather and lemons. In an instant an image of the figure in the mirror leered up at Caro and it took all her will power to push it away.

'Ugh!' said Albie, holding his nose.

'Intruder, possibly male, wears strong-smelling cologne,' the policeman confirmed, reading from his notebook scribbles.

'But why was he in my room? What was he looking for? Was he a Snake?' asked Caro. She remembered the headlines of the papers on the Flask Walk news stand. Hadn't they said the Snakes were infiltrating Hampstead?

'Got anything valuable?' asked the policeman looking at Gam. 'Diamonds? Pearls?'

'My pearls are still in their case,' said Gam. 'And

I've checked the silver candlesticks, and the vase my grandmother gave me. And my wedding ring. All present and correct.'

Wedding ring? Caro flashed a look at Albie. He looked as surprised as she was. She couldn't imagine prickly old Gam being married to anyone.

Gam was still talking, 'That's all we have of value. And it's all here. Nothing taken.'

'Won't be the Snakes then,' said the policeman confidently. 'They know what they're doing, believe me. If it was them, your pearls and what-not would be long gone.'

'Change the locks, Mrs Monday,' said the second policeman. 'Keep your eyes peeled. Telephone us and we'll be round straight away if there are any further developments.'

* * *

'Caroline,' said Gam after the police had gone and they were beginning to make their way back to bed. 'Wait a minute.'

Caro stopped as Gam caught up with her on the stairs. Awkwardly she rested a hand on Caro's shoulder. 'Well done today,' she said gruffly. Her eyes met Caro's and in that brief moment they looked kind. 'It must have been very frightening,' she added.

Caro nodded. It was the first time she had heard Gam speak without a sharp edge to her voice, and it made her feel a little bit trembly.

'Try not to worry,' Gam went on. 'We'll do our best to keep you safe.'

Caro watched as Gam made her way up the stairs ahead of her, her left hand on the banister, her right clutching the green silk umbrella.

Something about the way she moved made Caro feel sad. Like the weight of the world was on her shoulders.

But this was the woman who had driven her mother away. Who didn't believe in the concept of freedom. Who practically kept her and Albie under lock and key.

Gam was Gam.

Caro wouldn't allow herself to be taken in by her.

It was not what her mother would have wanted.

Chapter Seven

The next day the new nanny arrived after breakfast.

'Nanny's here, Mary!' called Marks brightly from the hall.

Then everyone nearly fell off their chairs when Marks came in, followed not by a Mary Poppins-type person, but by a real, live man.

His name was Tom and he won everyone over immediately – even Gam, once she had got over the initial shock.

'You remind me of someone,' she said, looking at him curiously. He had an abundance of bright red hair, merry grey-green eyes and the most muscly arms Caro had ever seen.

Tom said, 'Really?' in an eager sort of way. But then Gam had become preoccupied with smoothing the folds on her umbrella and said, 'Not now, not now,' and started to tell him about the rules of the house instead.

Tom listened carefully. Then he said, 'Mrs Monday, I can't nanny these children if they are kept indoors all day every day. You have employed me to care for them, and I will, but I would like to do it my way. And that means being in the great outdoors.'

Caro and Albie's mouths dropped open. Marks looked on admiringly.

A long minute stretched out as Gam assessed Tom silently.

'Very well then,' she said. 'If you give me your word to keep them safe.'

Caro and Albie goggled eyes at each other. How was it possible that this Tom had managed to get Gam to agree to that? Because he was a grown-up? Because he had special powers? 'Charm,' Marks said later. Released from her child-care duties, she had suddenly become a lot more cheerful.

* * *

On that first day, the three of them, Albie, Tom and Caro, strode about on the heath for hours. They played hide and seek, swam in the pond (ice-cold and full of slippery, slimy weeds, but still thrilling) and had a picnic.

Tom was a bit like Horace in that he loved to chat. They covered a range of subjects including their favourite foods (much to Albie and Caro's horror, Tom chose spinach, which he claimed was good for building muscles); books they had read more than five times, and who was best singer, Buddy Holly or Elvis Presley.

'D'you want to see something?' asked Caro on a whim. And she and Albie took Tom up to the Wilds and they showed him the site of the gym, and then, on a hunch (and because she was a good judge of character), Caro swore him to secrecy and told him about His Nibs.

'A rabbit!' he said

'Gam can't know, you mustn't tell her,' urged Albie.

'Your secret is safe with me,' he said.

And they could tell he meant it.

From that day on, things got better. Every day they managed to smuggle His Nibs out of the house; every day they went to the heath with Tom. After lunch, Tom would sit on a bench on Parliament Hill and read.

Then Albie and Caro would dash off to the Wilds, meet Horace, and get on with building the gym.

Albie thrived. The timid look had vanished. He was no longer pale, but rosy-cheeked. He treated Caro and Horace as if they were his older brother and sister. Horace, who was already a big brother to little Edwin, took it in his stride. But for Caro, being looked up to, being adored, was something new. She liked it when Albie said 'Can I?' and 'Should I?' and she got great pleasure from always saying 'Yes!'

Even better, Caro never heard him whimpering at night any more. He laughed a lot and he made Caro and Horace laugh too.

Victor also got into the habit of meeting them in the Wilds. He liked building things. He was full of suggestions about how to construct the balancing beam, and he helped them drag a fallen tree trunk that Horace had found near the ponds all the way up to the construction site. He showed them how to saw it to just the right size and plane it so it was smooth and straight. The planing took ages and it made their arms ache. But Victor promised that when it was ready, he would show them how to cut a mortise and tenon joint with a sharp chisel so that they could mount it between the tree and the tree stump and it would hold firm.

Of the three of them, it was Albie who turned out to be especially good at constructing. It must have been all that practice with the knitting needles, Caro joked. He listened carefully and was easily the one who could plane the longest without complaining. Horace worked hard too, but in all honesty, he preferred to sit with his back against the tree stump and knit, perfecting a variety of stitches with the wool and needles that Albie fetched from the house. Over the course of a couple of days he produced a snug pink waistcoat for His Nibs, and very long, very stripy scarves for Albie, Caro and Victor.

Meanwhile Caro kept them all entertained with her gymnastics, walking in ever decreasing circles on her hands, turning cartwheels and climbing all the climbable trees. She liked Victor enormously, not only because he adored His Nibs – bringing him luminous bundles of chickweed that he gathered on his walks to and from the heath – but because he was kind.

Always, he would make time to ask her quietly, 'OK?' and she would say, 'Just about,' because that was the truth. She *was* happier in Hampstead with the arrival of Tom; and Horace coming every day; and playing big sister to Albie. But of course the yearning for home – real home – never went away, even though Ronnie rang regularly and reassured her that everything would be all right, and that the consulate in Manaus was doing everything possible to track down her mum. But it was the longest Jacinta had ever been away, and even though Caro tried her very best to be reassured, it was hard.

While they worked, Victor boiled water in his tin can for tea and told them stories. They especially loved the ones about the tramps' secret language: chalk markings on gateposts and walls, a kind of code, indicating things like whether the inhabitants of a village were friend or foe. If no chalk could be found, a lump of coal or a scratchy nail would do. A circle with a dot inside it spelled danger. An upside-down V with a line across the top meant the household were exceptionally friendly and would provide a hot meal. When he first told them this, Caro stopped hammering and exclaimed out loud. There was an upside-down V marked on the post outside the pub!

'You live in a friendly establishment, then,' said Victor, his eyes twinkling. 'Kind to travelling folk,' he added. And Caro nodded, thinking of the bowls of roast potatoes Ronnie set aside, the slices of cold ham and beef that were sent out without question if a tramp passed by.

'I'm going to be a tramp when I grow up,' Albie announced. He, more than any of them, loved to listen to Victor's stories.

But instead of smiling and encouraging Albie, Victor's face became grave, and Caro glimpsed a flicker of sadness behind his kind eyes.

'I wouldn't recommend it, young chap,' he said.

'Why not? You get on all right!'

Victor started to pack up the tea things. No one said anything for a moment and the silence stretched awkwardly.

'Most of us gentleman travellers are on the road because we've had hard times,' he said at last. 'There are some men who lost everything in the war. Others had family difficulties. We've gone on the road to escape the things we had trouble dealing with. But...' He paused and scratched his beard and sighed. 'You *can't* escape it. It's still there, in your dreams, in your very bones.' He sighed again. The longest sigh Caro had ever heard. 'What I'm trying to say, young Albie, is, if you have a problem, face up to it, don't think you can deal with anything by running away.'

Thoughtfully he stroked His Nibs between the ears and then said so quietly that only Caro heard, 'You see, that's what I did, and I regret it every day.'

* * *

Life at Heath View was improving too. Gam seemed to be softening. Tom had taught them a new word: *idiosyncratic*. He thought that was what Gam was – a bit peculiar but generally harmless – and even Caro was starting to agree.

One day she had even encouraged them all to sit in the lounge with her after supper. They'd watched *Dixon of Dock Green* on the television, and afterwards Albie had raced upstairs and brought down armfuls of knitting needles and they'd played pick-up sticks until bedtime. Gam had even smiled once or twice, and she'd ruffled Albie's hair when he'd said goodnight.

But then something terrible happened.

And after that, everything changed.

* * *

It started the day the household woke to thunderous grey clouds and the steady pelt of rain.

'I've got errands to run,' said Gam at breakfast, tapping the floor with the tip of her green umbrella in a business-like manner. 'I shall be out for the best part of the day. Tom, with the weather as it is, I think you'd better stay indoors. There's plenty to do in the nursery.'

As soon as Gam left, Tom announced that he had plans. They would play pirates, he explained. The rules were that nobody's feet could touch the floor – and if they did, they were out. If there was nothing to grab hold of within stretching distance, they could lie on their backs with their legs and arms in the air and shuffle between pieces of furniture.

It was the most thrilling game that Caro had ever played and she was in her element. They leapt about, from table to chair, to bookcase, to bed, dragging themselves up the banisters, or sliding down to get between floors. The house shook with shrieks and shouts of laughter and they were so engrossed that nobody heard the front door slam shut. Albie was just gearing up to make the jump from piano to drinks cabinet when the drawing-room door flew open, and there stood Gam, returning unexpectedly for a forgotten purse.

'Albert Brown, what on earth do you think you are doing?' she demanded.

The others, who had been making encouraging whoops, froze; Caro was halfway up the curtains; Tom, blushing a dark shade of beetroot, started to explain.

But Gam wasn't listening. She was no longer looking at Albie. Her entire being was transfixed on something on the other side of the room. Her eyes bulged. Her hand clutched at her black-clad chest. And then, just as in the horror films when the star comes face to face with a monster or a ghost, she opened her mouth and let out a blood-curdling scream.

Caro followed her great-aunt's gaze and felt a thump of dread. Gam was pointing her wavering umbrella, not at a terrifying ghoul, but at His Nibs, who had hopped from the armchair to the mantelpiece, where he was now happily absorbed in munching a carrot top. He stared back at Gam contentedly, seemingly unaware that the screaming had anything to do with him.

Caro looked from the rabbit back to Gam and her mouth went dry. Albie had warned her what might happen if her great-aunt found out about His Nibs.

Even so, the look on her face was a hundred times worse than she had ever imagined.

'No animals in this house,' screeched Gam, her umbrella trembling, her eyes wild. 'Take it away! Take it away now!'

'Stop it!' said Albie, his face crumpling. 'Don't . . .'

'It's all right, Albie,' said Caro, scrabbling down the curtain and rushing over to place herself between the umbrella and the rabbit. 'It's only His Nibs,' she said to Gam. 'He won't cause any trouble, I promise!'

'You!' said Gam, backing out of the room, holding her umbrella in front of her as if for protection. 'Did *you* bring this creature into my house?'

Albie and Caro stared open-mouthed as Gam stumbled out of the door. They could hear her breathing, shallow, panicked breaths.

'Is she ... frightened, Caro?' whimpered Albie.

'Mrs Monday,' said Tom, following her out. 'Let me help ...'

'Marks!' Gam bellowed from the hall, waving him away with her umbrella. 'Telephone the RSPCA now.'

What?

'No!' shouted Caro, running out after her. 'Nothing's wrong with him. Why would you do that?'

'What's the matter?' yelled Marks, thundering down the stairs, her paintbrush in her hand. 'Tom? Mary?'

'If that rabbit isn't out of the house by the time I get back, I'll ... Shut the door, Tom! Shut it now so it can't get out!' Gam was taking great big gulping breaths that sounded like death gasps.

'Mary, please don't worry,' said Tom, closing the drawing-room door gently behind him. 'Don't you remember ...'

Gam turned on him furiously. 'Remember what? How dare you! I trusted you to look after my charges...' Her eyes swept over Caro and Albie. 'And instead you are playing silly games indoors. Harbouring a rabbit – not to mention destroying my furniture. I've a mind to give you your marching orders... Marks, don't tell me you knew, too?'

'Well...' said Marks.

'But I don't understand,' cut in Caro. Had Gam once been attacked by a rabbit? Was that even possible? What else could explain her reaction? 'He doesn't mean any harm. We'll keep him out of your way.'

'I will not, I will *not* have him here,' said Gam, her voice shaking. 'Tom, there is a cage in the shed at the bottom of the garden. Put him in there. Marks, if you're not going to make the call, I shall.'

They all watched as she disappeared into her study, heard her dial a number and then have a quiet conversation.

'Unfortunately they can't come until tomorrow,' said Gam as she reappeared in the hall. 'I'll give them until midday, but if they're not here by lunchtime, you'll have to let him loose on the heath.' She was still breathing heavily, her chest rising and falling in a steady rhythm.

Let him loose on the heath? Was she mad?

All of Caro's fledgling thoughts about Gam not being as bad as Jacinta had said she was flew away.

She wasn't idiosyncratic. She was just plain awful.

Now she knew her mother had been right all along.

'THAT is cruel,' she yelled, her voice cracking under the weight of worry. 'He's not used to being in the wild. A fox will get him. And I'll *die* if that happens. I will, I'll die.'

'Don't be so dramatic,' said Gam coldly. Now that there was distance between herself and His Nibs and the door was shut, she was beginning to recover her poise.

'You,' she said to Tom, 'may stay in post for now, but *that thing*' – she pointed her umbrella at the door – 'must be safely in the cage by the time I get back. And off the premises by midday tomorrow. Understood?'

Tom and Marks nodded. Caro stared mutinously at the ground. Albie looked at them all with shocked eyes.

Gam picked up her purse from the sideboard and rapped her umbrella twice on the floor.

'And, Tom, when the children are inside I expect them to be well-behaved, not tearing about all over the place like wild animals. This endless gallivanting on the heath seems to have put ideas into their heads. Too much freedom, that's the problem. I don't agree with it and it's gone on for too long.'

Chapter Eight

After Gam had gone, they stood in the hall quite shaken into silence. The calm after the storm, thought Caro. Except it was an extremely ominous calm. A calm with a very dangerous current running beneath it.

Caro hugged His Nibs to her. He was very still.

'It's all right,' she said to him. 'You've done nothing wrong.'

She remembered the nightmare thought she'd had, when she'd first arrived at Heath View. How she'd imagined a piece of invisible elastic connecting her and His Nibs, and what would happen if that piece of elastic snapped in two and, just like that, suddenly, violently, they were flung apart. She held the rabbit close and felt his heart pitter-pattering next to hers. She felt hot and panicky and a bit tearful. Gam's reaction had frightened her.

Albie looked terrified too.

'I told you, didn't I?' he whispered.

'But how can she hate rabbits so much?' she said. 'What have they ever done to her?'

Tom and Marks exchanged a look.

'What?' Caro said. 'Tell me!'

'She's just old,' said Tom.

'And finicky,' said Marks.

'You're always making excuses for her. Aren't they, Albie?'

'People who hate animals are horrid,' he agreed, and Caro gave him a weak smile, glad to have an ally.

They went out into the pouring rain and, sure enough, in the shed at the back of the garden was a rusty old cage.

'How come she's got that?' asked Caro.

'It's like she's the witch in Hansel and Gretel,' said Albie. 'The one who lived in a gingerbread house and locked children in a cage while she fattened them up.'

'That's not helping, Albie,' said Marks firmly.

'But what are we going to do?' asked Caro as Tom

ran a damp cloth over the cage and Albie fetched the hay from upstairs. They found a space for it under a dense tree so that it was almost sheltered from the rain. Why were Tom and Marks acting so strangely? Why weren't they as angry as she was about what had just happened? Even Albie seemed to have gone quiet. His face had that pointy look that she hadn't seen in ages.

'I'll think of something. I'll come up with a plan for you, my darling,' she said to His Nibs as she allowed Tom to take him from her and place him in the cage. 'No need to worry, all right?'

* * *

But Caro did worry, for the rest of the morning and all through lunch, which was an extremely subdued affair of macaroni cheese and baked tomatoes. Afterwards, Tom said he had to go out and run his own errands. Marks, trying to cheer them up, offered Albie and Caro an art lesson.

'I'll teach you how to paint like an old master,' she said brightly.

But Caro didn't see how on earth she could be expected to learn art techniques when Gam's threat was hanging so perilously over His Nibs.

She had to do something, take action. But what? Could she ask Horace to look after him? Not really. Mrs Braithwaite was allergic to the slightest hint of fur. Could she run away? Go back to the pub? What would Ronnie say? And would Toby's mum allow it?

'Come on, Caro,' said Albie, holding a hand out to her. 'It'll be all right.'

Did he really think that? She didn't see how it could be. And he'd had first-hand experience of Gam getting rid of his pets.

'I'll be up in a minute,' she said.

'Promise?' he said.

'Promise,' she said.

Of course she didn't go up. Instead, she went outside, where the rain had turned to drizzle and everything was sodden. His Nibs, crouched in the corner of the rusty old cage, munched disconsolately on a cabbage leaf. A steady drip from the laurel bush bounced off the wire mesh, sending a spray of tiny droplets in all directions. One of the droplets landed on his ear and he twitched it irritably.

Caro lifted the lid off the cage and scooped him up. His fur was damp and he seemed to shiver. Holding him close, she ran to the front of the house, dragged the pram out from its hiding place and gently lowered him into it. There was still a fine covering of hay scattered across the bottom and a bedraggled mound of chickweed in the corner. She took off her jumper and covered him with it to keep him warm.

'Where have you been?'

Startled, Caro glanced up.

It was Horace, looking quite angry.

She had forgotten she was meant to be meeting him up in the Wilds that afternoon. They had intended to do some more work on the beam.

She flew into his arms.

'I'm sorry,' she said, 'but it's been dreadful, you'll never believe...'

'What happened?' said Horace, disentangling himself. He didn't go in much for hugs.

And Caro told him all about how heartless Gam was and how, if her threat was carried out and His Nibs was set loose on the heath, she wouldn't be able to breathe and... The words tumbled out and Horace listened to it all with great attention and sympathy, as friends do.

'I wish I could look after him for you, Caro,' he said when she had finished, 'but you know Mum...'

They stood looking at the rabbit, who had stopped shivering now and seemed quite comfortable, happy even, to be the centre of attention. But he wouldn't be happy for much longer. Not if Gam's threat was carried out.

Ronnie would say: 'I told you so,' and 'That's why I said Toby should look after him in the first place.' Perhaps, Caro thought, Ronnie had known about Gam's animal aversion all along.

But Caro could never have let Toby look after him! He would've forgotten to feed him! And he wouldn't have shown him any love.

She made a decision. She would telephone Ronnie. Confess. Try to win her round. Explain why she couldn't live at Heath View one minute longer. Surely she'd understand?

'I'm coming back to Waterloo, Horace,' she said determinedly. 'I'll *beg* Toby's mum to let me stay at the pub if I have to. She can't turn me away, can she? It's my home.'

* * *

They agreed that Horace would guard His Nibs while Caro sneaked back into the house to fetch her suitcase and telephone Ronnie. Then they would collect Jacinta's tools from the hollow of the tree and head back to Waterloo.

As she slithered into the house via a downstairs window, Caro wondered what to do about Albie. He would be upstairs with Marks having his art lesson. She'd promised to follow him up there and she didn't, as a rule, break her promises.

But if you were running away, you didn't just burst in and announce your departure, did you? Marks would be bound to stop her, then she'd tell Gam and ...

By the time Caro had reached the telephone, which was halfway up the stairs, she had made a decision. Albie would be better off here. With Tom and Marks to look after him and everything going on as normal. Besides, hadn't he just got that pinched look about him again? She couldn't risk saying goodbye. He was bound to make a fuss. He might even cry.

The telephone was a large black contraption, old-fashioned, bigger than the one they had in the pub. Caro stretched out a hand to pluck up the receiver, but before she was able to grasp hold of it, it started to ring. Maybe this was Ronnie ringing now! She did ring most days.

Caro lifted the receiver and held it to her ear.

'Hello?' she said.

There was silence on the other end of the line and then a sniff.

Not Ronnie, then.

'Hello?' Caro said again.

The line crackled and then: 'Put it back where you found it or there'll be trouble.' The voice was muffled and monotone, but distinctly male.

'What?' asked Caro into the mouthpiece. 'What're you talking about?'

But whoever it was had said what they wanted to say. A click, and then all that remained was the flat buzz of the dialling tone.

Carefully Caro replaced the receiver onto its cradle. A sliver of fear flicked up her spine. Put *what* back or there'd be trouble? And what *sort* of trouble did the person mean?

It was just like all that stuff she'd heard on the radio, about that gang, the Snakes. *They* made threatening phone calls to people.

But she didn't have anything that didn't belong to her, did she? The call must be meant for someone else ... maybe Gam or Marks, or ... Tom?

Downstairs the front door slammed. Caro stepped away from the phone.

She could hear the familiar tap, tap of the umbrella on the hall floor. Gam was back. Bother. And she was coming upstairs.

In a flash, Caro hopped across the landing, yanked open Tom's bedroom door and slipped inside. Gam wouldn't come in here. Caro would hide until the coast was clear, and then she'd scarper.

While she waited and listened to Gam tapping her way upstairs, Caro surveyed Tom's room with interest. It was a pleasant room with a curtain of leaves swaying outside the window, giving it a peaceful air, and everything very neat. Not like Marks's room, which looked like a bomb had hit it, with paints and make-up and jewellery strewn all over the place. Tom had actually made his bed with hospital corners; his books were lined up in order of size and a perfectly folded pile of clean washing lay on the chair in the corner.

Caro scanned the long, low bookshelf that ran beneath the window. *The World's Best Boys' Annual*; *Tales of Pluck and Peril for Boys and Girls*.

Children's books. But Tom wasn't a child. She ran her fingers along their cracked spines. The books were old. She picked up one of the annuals and sniffed it. That musty, old-book smell. A smaller slim book dropped out of the bigger one onto the floor.

How to Care for Your Rabbit.

That was odd, considering Gam's reaction this morning.

Or maybe it wasn't so odd. Something had happened to Gam, thought Caro. Something to do with a rabbit that had turned her against them. And yet here was this book, and out in the garden was an ancient hutch.

She plucked the book up and flicked through it. The usual stuff: what to feed them, how to build a hutch, tips on grooming. The pictures were nice and it was just the right size to fit in a jeans pocket, so Caro tucked it into hers.

Along the corridor, she heard a door open and close. Good. Gam had shut herself inside her bedroom. This was Caro's chance. Quick as she could, she fled upstairs and shoved everything into her suitcase. She swung her cape over her shoulders, plucked the little bird painting out from under her pillow, wrapped it up in some newspaper and tucked it into a small pocket that Horace had sewn inside the lining.

It was the perfect fit.

Swiftly, she raced downstairs and out of the front door. The gravel on the drive crunched noisily but she didn't stop and she didn't look back.

On the other side of the road, Horace and His Nibs were waiting.

'What did Ronnie say?' asked Horace.

Caro stopped, realising that in her rush she'd forgotten to phone her. Too late now. She'd have to do it when she got to Waterloo.

'Didn't get round to it. Come on!' she said. And, with Horace and Caro taking it in turns to pull and push the pram, the three of them bumped their way across the heath.

They were a short distance from the Wilds when Caro came to an abrupt stop.

Someone was whistling. Whistling a tune that was so familiar, Caro's heart seemed to fly into her mouth.

It wasn't 'The Flower Duet', was it?

It was! Floating across the heath, spiralling round and round. High and wild and sweet and . . .

'Caro, why've you stopped? What's the matter?' asked Horace.

'Listen!' she said.

Horace retraced his steps until he was standing next to her and visibly cocked an ear.

'I can't hear anything,' he said

But Caro was away. Running in the direction of the whistling, as fast as her legs could carry her, her chest hammering, her heart pounding, across the heath and towards the Wilds. It was her mother! It had to be! Somehow, she'd known Caro would be here. She'd come to get her! And now everything was going to be all right.

But as quickly as it had come, the whistling stopped, and Caro, unable to follow the sound any longer, lurched to a halt. She closed her eyes and listened with all her might. Birdsong; the rustle of leaves in trees; the drip of raindrops.

But no whistling.

Had she imagined it? Had she yearned for this moment for so long that her mind had played tricks on her?

'Look!' cried Horace from somewhere behind her.

Caro turned and her mouth dropped open. Horace was standing on the balancing beam and she saw that it was finished, stretching in a clean line from one tree stump to the other.

In a great rush, Caro wrenched off her shoes and sprang onto it. The wood felt smooth and strong, with just the hint of a spring. She walked the length of it on her hands, and then returned in three perfect cartwheels. She pointed her right foot and in one elegant movement stepped forward, raised her arms and pushed herself into a handstand; she held the position, counting under her breath all the way up to ten, then flipped over into a crab and sprang up again.

'Bravo!' shouted Horace, clapping wildly.

'It must've been Victor,' said Caro as she jumped down, her eyes shining. 'He must've come up here this morning and finished it in the rain, and...' A thought struck her, one that was not half as joyful, '... but now I'm leaving I won't be able to thank him.'

Or show him what she was capable of.

'We'll come back, Caro, 'course we will!' said Horace encouragingly as he watched her face fall.

But would they?

Caro had barely allowed herself to imagine bringing Jacinta and Ronnie up here and introducing them to her new friends, Albie and Tom and Marks and Victor. But she knew she *had* hoped for it. Secretly. To see their pride, to show them how well she had managed until today.

'Yes,' she said. 'We *will* come back.' And for a moment she believed they would.

Because otherwise ... well ... all this work for nothing? It didn't seem right, somehow.

Chapter Nine

By the time Caro and Horace emerged from the tube at Waterloo, dusk was falling.

'Meet you in the Rubbles later?' she called as the two of them parted ways.

'You bet,' Horace yelled, adjusting his beret and dancing off down the street. He could scarcely conceal his delight at having his friend back on home turf.

When Caro turned the corner and saw the lights of the pub shining behind the leaded windows and heard the chatter and caught the familiar smells of business as usual, her heart swelled as if it might burst.

She had missed it *so* much.

'Why, it's young Caro,' murmured the locals as she

swung pink-cheeked through the door, dragging the pram behind her, and setting her case down with a thud. She stood for a moment, drinking it all in: the polished wood of the bar, the pint glasses glinting above it in neat rows, the glow of the dusky pink fringed lamps, the red leatherette stools, the bottles of wines and spirits, the three kinds of beer on tap. A fug of smoke mingling with a sort of saltiness filled the air – a blend of cigarettes and Smiths Crisps.

The only things missing, she thought with a pang, were Ronnie and Mum.

'Caro!' It was Toby, serving behind the bar, his face flushed, his quiff gone flat. He finished pulling a pint and set it down. He was actually smiling at her, as though he was pleased to see her, and she wasn't sure but, as his gaze took in the pram and her suitcase, it seemed like a look of relief flitted across his features. 'You're back.'

Caro hadn't expected to get such a warm welcome from Toby. And she realised with surprise that she was quite happy to see him, too.

'What're you doing serving?' she asked. That was usually Ronnie's job and surely now it was Emerald Standing's. Plus, Toby had never shown much of an inclination to help before.

'Well, you know . . .' said Toby vaguely.

Caro didn't know, but then another customer called for his attention, and so she carried on nodding hello to the regulars as she moved through the bar. By the fire, two men in black leather jackets lounged in the best velvet chairs with their legs stuck out in front of them. New customers, thought Caro. Ronnie would be pleased. More customers meant more money in the till, and perhaps, one day, another holiday for them all.

She nodded to the leather-jacketed men and they nodded civilly back. One of them had the kind of shiny, rock-hard quiff that Toby could only dream of; the other had an exceptionally bushy moustache.

'Where's your mum?' she asked Toby, when he had finished serving. She would settle His Nibs in a minute. He'd be pleased to see his hutch again. But first she had to get Emerald Standing on her side.

'In the kitchen,' he said. His smile had gone, and now he looked anxious, his eyes flitting nervously from side to side. 'But she's busy at the moment . . . doing the accounts . . .'

Caro knew all about the accounts. When Ronnie did them, she closeted herself away and wasn't to be disturbed *unless someone's dying*. 'I need to concentrate!'

she'd say. 'I'll go wrong and have to start adding up all over again.'

But today Caro couldn't wait. She had to get this over with: ask Mrs Standing immediately if she could stay, and then maybe (an irrational thought) there'd be less chance of her saying 'no'.

Ignoring Toby, she pushed the pram containing His Nibs through the beaded curtains and into the kitchen. It was a bright, cheerful place, with a row of plants lined up on the windowsill and blue-and-white patterned crockery piled high on the shelves. At the centre of it, an extremely sophisticated-looking woman was sitting at the kitchen table, smoking a cigarillo and tapping a great quantity of ash into Ronnie's favourite gold-rimmed saucer.

'Who on earth are you?' she asked as Caro entered. She looked a bit like the women in the magazines that Horace liked to read, in a leopard-print dress, with shiny coils of coal-black hair arranged in a complicated fashion on top of her head.

'And what,' she continued, raising her perfectly arched eyebrows, 'is in there?'

'I'm Caro,' said Caro as politely as she could. 'And this is His Nibs. He lives in the hutch outside.' She hefted the rabbit out of the pram and nodded towards the door that led out to the yard. It was wide open, and just then a gust of cold air blew in.

'You're Mrs Rudd's charge?' said Emerald Standing, rising to her feet. She was tall, much taller than Ronnie, and made the kitchen seem rather small. 'So you must be the one,' she said, after a moment's pause, 'who is rather good at climbing.'

Caro blinked and pride bloomed. Had Toby told her that? Perhaps things were off to a good start. Much better than when she'd first met Gam.

'I am,' she said. 'As soon as I'm sixteen I'm going to—'

'But what are you doing here?' interrupted Emerald Standing, looking puzzled. 'I thought it was understood that you'd be staying somewhere north of the river?'

'I was,' said Caro. She released His Nibs and watched as he bounded outside. Then all in a rush she added, 'I came to ask, could I come back? Stay here? I won't be any trouble. It's just ... His Nibs ... wasn't welcome in the other place.'

The request was barely out of her mouth when the beaded curtain parted and Toby appeared.

'What?' said Mrs Standing, not particularly kindly, Caro thought.

'Sorry, Mum,' he said in a squirming way that made

Caro wince. 'I tried to tell her you were busy, but she wouldn't listen.'

Toby was clutching her suitcase. 'I'll take it up for you,' he said when he saw her looking at it, and then he gave that strange nervy smile of his again.

'No, thank you,' she said firmly. She couldn't remember him offering to help with anything before. He'd always had to be *told*.

She turned back to Mrs Standing, who had started to tap her long crimson fingernails on the kitchen counter. Her black eyeliner flicked up elegantly at the corner of each eye and her mouth was pursed.

In the doorway Toby shifted nervously from foot to foot. He seemed rather jumpy, Caro thought.

'For goodness' sake, lad, stop twitching,' said Mrs Standing impatiently. 'Put the girl's case down like she asked you to and carry on serving – please.'

When Toby had sloped off, she turned back to Caro. 'But Mrs Rudd was clear—'

'I'm begging of you!' said Caro. She was actually clasping her hands together. If Emerald said no, what would she do? She couldn't go back now.

Emerald Standing stared at her and frowned. 'I'm not here to be a mother,' she said.

'Apart from to Toby,' Caro reminded her.

'Yes,' said Emerald. A flicker of irritation passed over her features. Caro didn't blame her. Who in their right mind would want to be Toby's mum?

'Honest,' Caro tried again, 'You won't even notice I'm here, cross my heart.'

Mrs Standing regarded her for a long, keen moment. 'Do you promise not to cause any trouble? Stay out of my way? Take care of yourself?' she said.

'Promise,' Caro said.

'Don't make me regret it,' said Emerald.

'You won't,' said Caro.

Mrs Standing was all sharp edges. Brittle. Cold. Yet her demands that Caro stay out of her way and take care of herself were music to Caro's ears. The complete opposite to Gam and her silly, over-the-top rules.

She thought about Tom, and Albie and Marks. They had probably realised she'd gone by now. What would they think? A tiny part of her felt guilty that she had left without saying goodbye. But …

No point worrying about that now. She'd had to do it. To keep His Nibs safe. And if that meant tolerating the stern-faced Mrs Standing, it was still a million miles better than being back in Hampstead and waiting for Gam to carry out her terrible threat.

* * *

Less than an hour later, Caro and His Nibs were in the Rubbles. There was an unseasonal chill in the air and she drew the brown velvet cape tight round her shoulders. On the other side of the river, Big Ben chimed seven.

'Why's Horace taking so long? Surely he must've finished his tea by now?' she said to the rabbit. He gave an answering quiver, which looked as if he was shrugging his shoulders, and turned back to his dandelion leaf.

'Well, it doesn't matter, we can wait,' she said.

There was always lots to do in the Rubbles. First Caro collected a pile of bricks, and His Nibs looked on admiringly as she began to build a wobbly little wall. Then they swung together on the tyre swing, and after that His Nibs discovered a new patch of chickweed. When Big Ben struck eight, Caro sought out the pile of wood she'd been saving to build the gym with, and took some of the smaller bits to make a fire. In the boot of the car she rummaged around until she found a packet of marshmallows that she'd been saving for a special occasion. She stuck them on the ends of a few twigs and as the flames licked and leapt, began to toast them. His Nibs liked the fire. He snuggled up to Caro in a cat-like way and even did a sort of purr.

'Boo!' shouted Horace, making Caro scream and the rabbit jump. He was dressed in an extremely long black coat with the collar turned up. Where the coat swished the ground Caro could see a flash of blue-and-white striped pyjamas.

'It's the new look,' he said, striking a pose that made Caro laugh out loud. He was clutching his scrapbook and the newspaper Victor had given him a few days ago.

'No, really, I had to sneak out. Mum thinks I'm in bed,' he said. Mrs Braithwaite was notoriously strict about bedtimes. 'Luckily she had the telly on full blast. Listening to stuff about that ballerina – what's-her-name, you know, Margot Fonteyn – getting arrested in Panama. But I've left the back door unlocked so it'll be easy to sneak back in later.'

Horace stuck his head in the boot of the car. He fished out a pair of scissors and a small bottle of glue.

The fire crackled, the sky darkened, and the marshmallows – toasted until they went caramelised – tasted delicious. Horace snipped with his scissors and stuck his cuttings into his scrapbook. His Nibs snoozed, and Caro lay on her back and looked up at the stars.

It was just like old times.

Except it wasn't.

Mum was still missing and, Caro realised with a sudden jolt, she still hadn't got round to phoning Ronnie. That mysterious telephone call at Heath View had put her off her stride. Bother. What if Ronnie phoned Hampstead tonight before Caro had a chance to get her side of the story in first?

'Horace,' she said, jumping up. 'I've got to go back to the pub. I forgot to ring Ronnie earlier, and—'

'Sssh,' hissed Horace. 'Can't you hear that?'

Nearby something crunched. Caro reached out for His Nibs, pulled him close. The distinct sound of someone muttering. Then a stumble.

'Who is it?' she whispered to Horace. Not the Bully Boys, surely, coming to spoil their fun?

'Caro!' wavered a voice uncertainly. 'Where are you? I know you're here somewhere!'

Chapter Ten

It was Albie, appearing out of the darkness like an apparition. He was dressed as if he was going on a very long journey, with an old-fashioned rucksack on his back, and he was holding a walking stick. A smaller version of Victor and his fellow gentlemen of the road.

'You left me on my own! Without even saying goodbye!' he burst out. 'How could you have gone off and not said anything?' There were dirty streaks down his cheeks where he'd been crying.

In the split-second decision made earlier today in Hampstead, Caro had convinced herself that Albie would be better off with Marks and Tom. Now it dawned on her that she'd been selfish, only thinking about herself and His Nibs. She hadn't properly considered the effect of her actions on Albie. And now here he was, having come halfway across town all on his own, and he wasn't even street savvy like her and Horace.

'I know you're both best friends,' continued Albie. 'Sticking together through thick and thin and all that.' He glared at them both. 'But ... I *never* have adventures.'

'I thought you didn't want adventures,' Caro muttered. But as soon as she said it she knew it to be untrue. The old Albie, the sad, pinched-faced Albie, had been frightened of adventures. The new Albie, the one who had blossomed since she had arrived; who had saved His Nibs by pretending to fall down the stairs when Gam had been on the brink of discovering him; who had escaped the house on his own to follow her and Horace to the heath; who had shown them the Wilds; who was enthralled by Victor's tales ... who was like a little brother to her ...

'Of course he wants adventures!' said Horace. 'Who wouldn't? And nice outfit by the way, Albs. Can I have a go with your stick?'

Albie handed the stick over and Horace tossed

it around like a baton twirler in a marching band. Albie giggled.

Horace always had a knack for saying the right thing, thought Caro. He saw the best in everyone.

'You're right,' she said. 'I was so worried I wasn't thinking properly...'

But a niggle remained... did Marks and Gam and Tom know he'd followed her, and would that get her into even more trouble?

'How did you find us?' asked Horace.

'I asked some boys.'

'Which boys?' Caro interjected.

'Greasy hair. Long jackets.'

'Oh, Albie!' exclaimed Caro. 'Why d'you have to do that!'

'Do what? What's wrong about it?' He looked like he was about to start crying again.

'You only went and asked our sworn enemies. Of all the stupid things...'

'Caro...' Horace touched her lightly on the shoulder. She shook him off.

'*That's* why I didn't ask you! You don't understand about this stuff. Any minute now, they'll be here ruining everything like they always do.'

Albie's face screwed itself up. His Nibs gave Caro

a look and hopped over to nuzzle Albie's ankles. Something about the rabbit's attention seemed to give Albie renewed strength.

'Fine,' he said. 'I actually came to tell you something I thought you'd like to hear. Something important. But if you're not interested, then that's your problem.'

Abruptly, he turned on his heel and started to stumble off into the darkness.

Horace and Caro looked at one another. Horace waggled his eyebrows. He was warning her, saying, Caro!? Go after him. Show some sympathy. He's too green to be out on his own.

Caro knew he was right. Albie had followed her halfway across London, after all.

Plus, she wanted to know what he had to say that was so important.

'Albie, stop!' she called out after him. 'I'm sorry. You weren't to know about the Bully Boys.'

Albie turned. Took a few steps back towards them, regarded her warily. 'Are you *really* sorry, Caro Monday?'

'Yes,' said Caro, wondering what she could offer as a token of peace. 'Do you want a toasted marshmallow? It's gone cold but it's still nice.'

Albie crouched down and accepted the proffered

marshmallow. He chewed it slowly and then ate another. Caro added a few more sticks to the fire and the flames leapt up, making flickering patterns of light and shadow.

'Those boys didn't follow me anyway,' said Albie. 'They were too busy queuing up to see *The Mummy*.'

Caro snorted. *The Mummy* was a horror film that all the older kids in the neighbourhood had seen. 'They won't get into that! They look way too young,' and she nudged Albie in the ribs to show that they were proper friends now, just like her and Horace, and he nudged her back.

'So, what did you want to tell us?' she asked.

Albie turned his rucksack upside down, and Caro and Horace watched as a torch, a small gas stove, very similar to Victor's, several tin plates and a crumpled mess of rope and knitting needles fell out and puddled on the ground.

'Before I realised you'd run away, and I was looking for you, I went into Tom's room and I found this,' he explained. From the mound of stuff, he plucked up a small glass bottle full of amber liquid and handed it to Caro.

The glass was cold in her hands. She turned it over so that she could read the label on the other side.

Russian Leather: Cologne for Men.

Caro looked from the bottle to Albie. What was he doing, going round stealing other people's cologne?

'Why are you looking at me like that? Smell it, then,' he said, a bit impatiently. In the light of what was left of the fire, his eyes gleamed.

Carefully, Caro unscrewed the cap and took a good, long sniff. And then reeled back as if it were poison.

It was the same leathery, lemony smell that had filled the air on the night of the intruder.

'What?' asked Horace. It was obvious something was wrong.

'It's the ... the same smell ...' Caro stuttered.

The ground seemed to shift beneath her feet.

Did that mean ...

'It's definitely Tom's?' she said to Albie. Albie nodded, his eyes wide.

Funny, nice Tom? Whom they all trusted?

Horace was looking from Albie to Caro and back again. 'Will someone please explain!' he said.

'The thing is,' she said, 'if this is Tom's cologne ...'

'Which it is!' interrupted Albie.

'Then *he* must've been the intruder.'

'The person who broke into your bedroom?' asked Horace. 'The one you saw in the mirror?'

Caro shuddered. 'Yes,' she said.

That meant he'd been in the house the night before he had 'officially' arrived. The thought was so horrible it gave her the shivers.

And if he *had* been the intruder, then might he have been the one who made the telephone call, too? The mystery person asking her to put something back?

The 'something' he had probably been looking for?

But how could she put something back if she hadn't taken anything!

Unless...

Caro stared at Horace and Albie as a thought struck her.

If Tom *had* been looking for something that night in her room, and the man on the phone – maybe Tom – thought she *had* taken something that didn't belong to her, the only thing she had that might possibly, potentially, be of any value was...

The painting.

She reached inside her brown velvet cape and felt for the inner pocket. Drew the painting out. Peeled away its newspaper wrapping.

There it was. The bird, all speckly brown, with

white-tipped feathers. The dark-pink blossom and the patches of pale-blue sky.

But it wasn't valuable!

Was it?

And she *hadn't* taken it from anywhere! It had just *been there* in the suitcase.

'Let's see!' Horace leaned towards her to get a good look, and as he did, he drew a sharp breath.

'What, Horace? Why are you looking like that?'

'That's—'

He picked up his scrapbook and furiously leafed through the pages until he got to the bit he was looking for. It was the page he had literally just finished sticking in an hour or so earlier: the front-page article from the newspaper that Victor had used as a pillow. The one showing Lady Dockitt wearing the party dress by Dior.

Horace reached for the painting and plucked it from Caro's grasp.

'Hey!' said Caro. 'Careful!'

Horace held the painting close. He squinted at it, as though he was some kind of art expert, and shone the torch at it, inches from its surface. 'Where d'you say you got it?' he said.

'I told you a million times! It was in Mum's suitcase!' said Caro.

'But it looks exactly like the one they describe here...'

'It can't be!' said Caro. She craned her neck to try and read the words that Horace was busy scanning.

'Listen,' he said. 'A bird painting... Old master... Extremely valuable... Stolen from a high-society couple... Lord and Lady Dockitt. Says they only discovered its disappearance a few days ago because they'd been away on a cruise. Lucky them, if only...'

'Stop!' said Caro. 'It must be a mistake. How could a stolen painting have got into Mum's suitcase? It doesn't make sense.'

'The artist is called Cornelis van Pieter,' continued Horace as if he hadn't heard her.

'Tons of people must paint birds,' said Albie, chipping in. 'Doesn't mean Cornelis whatchamacallit painted this one.'

'Albie's right,' agreed Caro enthusiastically. She didn't want her painting to be the stolen one. What on earth did that mean if it was?

'What's that, then?' said Horace, pointing at a squiggle in the bottom right-hand corner of the painting. He had his 'told you so' face on.

Caro and Albie looked. Saw the teeny-tiny initials. CVP.

'Uh-oh,' said Albie.

Caro's heart did a little flip.

'Listen to this!' exclaimed Horace. 'The police believe it to be the work of an *elusive gang* known as the Snakes.'

The Snakes. Just the word gave Caro a queasy feeling in the pit of her stomach.

Did that mean *Tom* was a Snake? A secret Snake slithering around Gam's house?

'So ... *is* it valuable?' asked Albie.

'Is it valuable?? It's worth trillions!' said Horace. He was holding the painting a lot more carefully now, with just his fingertips at the edges. He passed it back to Caro. 'Anything by an old master is.'

Caro stared at the painting. It must be very old as well as very valuable. How on earth had Tom known that it was in her possession? For she was certain that he must've known. That was why he had crept into her room in the dead of night while she lay sleeping. And when he hadn't succeeded in getting his hands on it, he had wormed his way into the household by posing as a nanny. Had he been waiting? Waiting like a snake in the grass for that perfect moment? To slither back into Caro's room and have another go? Maybe he was in there right now and ... when he realised she'd done a runner ...

'Albie,' she said, feeling all jittery. 'Does Tom know you've gone?'

'He thinks I'm in bed,' said Albie confidently. 'And I told him *you* had a headache. Gam doesn't know you've gone yet either. She came home with a bad back and went straight into her room and said not to be disturbed.'

'But what about Marks?' said Caro. Since Tom's arrival Marks had mellowed. Even so, she was still loyal to Gam. She was bound to raise the alarm.

'It's all taken care of!' said Albie. 'I left her a note: "*I know where Caro is. I've gone to get her and bring her back before Gam finds out. Please don't tell.*"' Albie recited proudly.

'But that's not true!' said Caro. 'I'm not going back!'

'I expect Albie was just buying time, right Albie?' interjected Horace. 'As long as you're back by breakfast, no harm done?'

'No harm done,' said Albie, giving Horace a grateful smile.

Caro examined the painting again. If the newspapers were saying the Snakes had stolen it, then how had it ended up in Jacinta's suitcase? Could it have been by accident? Or was it by design?

When Ronnie and mum argued – which wasn't very

often, but when they did – Ronnie always said, 'Think first, Jacinta! Think before you act!' Well, what if she hadn't thought properly this time?

Was *that* why she hadn't come home when she was meant to?'

'Think logically,' Ronnie would say when Caro got all worked up over nothing.

How *could* Jacinta be involved? Especially when she was thousands and thousands of miles away in South America.

Caro didn't want her mum to be mixed up in any Snakes business. They sounded horrible and dangerous.

'I think we should give it back,' she announced, 'to Lord and Lady whatchamacallit ...'

'Dockitt,' said Horace.

If she gave it back, then she could just forget all about it and go back to normal. If Tom still wanted it, he could go and stalk *them* instead of her.

'But how will you give it back? You can't just knock on their door and say, "Hello, here's your painting, thank you very much and goodbye,"' said Albie.

'They'll ask questions,' Horace agreed.

They were right. They would. And the questions would lead in all the wrong directions. Back to her mum's suitcase and what was the painting doing inside it in the first place. Caro pressed her fingertips to her temples and thought hard. Whatever your problem, there's always a solution, Ronnie said.

'Well, then,' she said as they waited expectantly. 'I'll have to smuggle it in.'

Chapter Eleven

The fire had died down and only a faint glow came from the embers now. The Rubbles was shrouded in darkness, the tyre swings and the dens just black hulks.

'Smuggle it in?' said Albie.

'I'll sneak it in when they're asleep. They'll wake up in the morning and it'll just be there. Da-nah! If *I* was them, I'd be really pleased.'

There was a silence while Horace and Albie made sense of what she had just proposed. They didn't look convinced.

'And how do you think you'll do that?' asked Horace, sounding for all the world like one of the teachers at South Square Secondary.

'How d'you think?' she said. 'You've seen me! I can climb up any building as long as there are a few footholds. I won't get caught.'

'But what if you *do* get caught?' said Horace. 'We'd get into terrible trouble. You'd be accused of burgling, Caro. And we'd be your accomplices.' He visibly shuddered. 'Mum would go mad.'

It's true Mrs Braithwaite wouldn't be very happy, thought Caro. She was strict like that.

'Why can't we just take it to the police?' suggested Albie.

'My thoughts exactly!' said Horace.

Underneath her cape, Caro crossed her arms. They were both acting so ... *sensibly*. They didn't seem to realise the jeopardy of the situation.

'We can't go to the police,' she said firmly. 'Number one, you've heard what the Snakes do to their enemies. If they find out we went to the police they'd ...' She mimed slitting her throat.

'But they'll do that anyway!' said Albie. 'When they find out we've given the painting back to the Dockitts.'

'What's number two, Caro?' asked Horace. He pushed his glasses up his nose and looked at her thoughtfully.

Caro felt a panicky sob rise up into her throat. She

gulped it back down. 'Don't you see? The police will think Mum is implicated. And she's not here to explain herself. It doesn't look very good, does it?'

Giving the painting back to the Dockitts was a much better bet. At least until Mum came home and was able to tell her side of the story.

'I can go alone,' she said defiantly. 'You two don't have to come with me.'

As if on cue, His Nibs left Albie's side and bounded back over to Caro. She reached down gratefully and tickled his ears. *He* would never let her down.

'If he's going, then I'm coming too,' said Horace. 'You won't catch me being upstaged by a rabbit!'

'Or me!' said Albie.

* * *

Thank goodness for Horace. He knew exactly where the Dockitts lived. He'd read all about it in *The Times*, on the Society pages. 'It's really swish,' he said with just a hint of envy. 'Claridge House. Fourth floor flat. On the corner. *And* they drive a gold-plated Rolls-Royce.' He collected his sketchbook and pencil from the boot of the car. 'If we've got time, I'd like to draw it.'

Caro wrapped the painting back up in its scrap of

newspaper and tucked it into the pocket Horace had sewn into the lining of the cape. Albie shoved his kit back into the rucksack. And then they set off.

It was properly dark now: black-dark, the streetlamps casting orangey-blue stripes across the pavement, the roads all ghostly without the people and the traffic. In Trafalgar Square, Nelson's Column stretched enticingly up into the star-studded sky. Any other time, Caro would've climbed aboard one of the fierce bronze lions and scuttled her way to the top.

Not tonight.

On they went, footsteps echoing, voices loud in the quiet night air, cutting behind the National Gallery, wiggling their way up through the back streets of Soho, out onto the wide sweep of Regent Street and over to Mayfair on the other side. The air was cold, nipping at their cheeks and noses. To keep warm they ran, weaving in and out and around each other, His Nibs bowling along beside them. Past Hanover Square, along Brook Street until they came to Davies Street and halfway down, Claridge House.

They clustered together in the shadow of an umbrella shop opposite. They observed that Claridge House was an extremely elegant-looking building; a sleek Rolls-Royce gleamed under the streetlamps outside.

'Look! Imagine driving that!' said Horace. He crossed over and gave the tyres an experimental kick and swept his hand along the bonnet admiringly. 'All the way to the south of France and back!'

'Sssh!' said Caro. It wasn't difficult to imagine a future sophisticated Horace, swanning about all over the place in a sports car. But there was no time to think about that now. She needed to concentrate. Carefully she examined the building with a practised eye. There were plenty of footholds and a conveniently situated drainpipe running up the left-hand side of the building. A few leaps across several window ledges and she would be in position. The corner flat had a large sash window. With any luck it wouldn't be locked.

'Keep a look-out,' she instructed. 'Don't let His Nibs follow me. And cause a diversion if anyone comes.'

The first part was easy: up the drainpipe, past the first floor, the second floor, and the third; at the fourth, she took a giant leap across to the nearest window ledge, landing without even a wobble. From here it was a short spring to the second window ledge. The curtains at both windows were closed. But when she hopped across to the third window ledge, the curtains were open, and she could see straight inside, to the remains of a meal at a long table: some sort of roast joint; a half-eaten jelly; a collection of dishes and spoons. Caro's mouth watered. The macaroni cheese they'd had at Heath View at lunchtime seemed like years ago. And all she'd had for tea were toasted marshmallows.

Amongst the tableware, something moved. An arrow of fear whizzed straight up Caro's body. But then she saw it was only a cat licking a bowl. He stopped, raised his little head, and stared straight at her, as though he was saying, 'Care to join me?' Caro clamped her hand over her mouth to bottle a spurt of hysterical laughter. Then she took one last leap and arrived at the window ledge of the Dockitts' flat.

Down below, the street was quiet. No one about except two faraway faces and a large rabbit. Caro waved; they waved back. Then she turned and heaved at the window. *Please let it be open.* She heaved again and – bravo! – without even a whisper, it slid up. Silently she crawled through and dropped down onto an extremely soft and luxurious carpet on the other side.

She was in a study, the streetlights from outside illuminating bookcases, a large desk, a leather armchair, the shapes of paintings on the walls. Caro stepped closer. The paintings were evenly spaced. Farmyard animals. A poppy field. And then ... a gap ... and a hook ... with nothing hanging from it.

Caro's spirits lifted. This was going to be even easier than she'd imagined. The gap must be where the bird painting belonged.

Quickly she felt inside her cape for the package containing the painting. But her fingers had barely grasped it when her nose gave an ominous sort of tickle and before she could help it, she sneezed. Not once, not twice, but three explosive times.

The door to the study flew open and the light flicked on.

A woman was standing in the doorway. A woman dressed in a ruffled satin dressing gown and slippers with pom-poms the size of tennis balls decorating the toes.

'Stay right where you are!' she commanded with great authority.

'But ...' started Caro. She badly needed a handkerchief. Her nose was dripping. She wiped it on her sleeve.

'You've got exactly five seconds to tell me what's going on or I shall call the police,' the woman announced. Her finger hovered threateningly over a shiny silver button set in the wall. 'They'll be here quicker than you can say Jack Robinson ... Roland!' she yelled over her shoulder. 'Roly, come quick and see what I caught!'

'Please, there's no need to call the police,' blurted out Caro. 'I can explain...'

A man appeared in the doorway. He was also dressed for bed, in a silk dressing gown and velvet slippers. He rubbed his eyes and tugged at his hair and stared at Caro in utter astonishment.

'Look Roly, she's just a kid!' the woman exclaimed.

'Please, there's no need to press that button,' implored Caro. If Ronnie found out she'd run away from Hampstead and broken into a house in Mayfair, all in one day, she would be even madder than Horace's mum, and that was saying something. Her mind raced. Could she save the situation? 'I know this looks odd, but I'm actually here to do a good turn.'

'By breaking and entering?' asked the woman in disbelief. 'Funny way of going about it, I'm sure.'

'The thing is—' started Caro.

Down in the street a car horn began to blare.

'Hell's bells,' muttered the man. 'That's my Roller. Keep watch, Doreen. I'll be back in a sec.'

'Sit down,' ordered the woman called Doreen as they listened to Roly's receding steps and a door slamming. 'That's it, sit where I can see you, and don't try any funny business.'

The chair was so huge that Caro's feet didn't touch the ground. It made her feel very small, and very unimportant.

'Honestly, there's nothing funny about it,' said Caro in desperation. 'I've come to put something back, not *take* it . . .'

'Shh,' commanded Lady Dockitt. 'Wait until Roly comes back.

Defeated, Caro flumped further down in her chair. One minute everything had been going so well and now . . .

A door slammed again and Lord Dockitt reappeared, holding a scared-looking Albie and an embarrassed Horace by the scruff of their collars. There was a thudding noise and His Nibs appeared behind them, looking the most startled Caro had ever seen.

'Found the little rascals in the car,' Lord Dockitt exclaimed to his wife. 'Must be her accomplices. Only gone and picked the lock! Tooting the hooter for all it was worth!'

'And a rabbit, if you please! Is he involved as well?' asked Lady Dockitt. If Caro had been asked to put a bet on it, she would've wagered that Lady Dockittt was finding the whole situation rather amusing. But she couldn't be entirely sure.

'He's mine and he's innocent, just like we are,' she said. And then to Horace she muttered furiously, 'What were you doing?'

He and Albie had somehow managed to make an already bad situation even worse. How *could* they have let themselves get caught?

'We were just trying to cause a diversion,' he said.

'Like you asked us to,' said Albie. 'We saw the light go on.'

'But I didn't mean...!'

'*And* we heard you sneeze,' said Horace.

It had all gone wrong. Now Lord and Lady Dockitt were going to ask questions. Endless questions. Caro would have to say she'd found the painting in her mum's suitcase, and they would assume Jacinta was a thief and they'd tell the police and then *she'd* be arrested as soon as she arrived home.

If she ever came home.

'They *do* start you young these days, don't they?' said Lord Dockitt.

'Miniature burglars,' nodded Lady Dockitt. 'Can't be more than ten.'

'We're not burglars!' said Caro. 'And I'm twelve, if you must know, and so is Horace, and Albie's—'

'Nine and four months,' said Albie.

'I do believe they were going to steal another painting, Roly,' said Lady Dockitt. 'Do you think they belong to the Snakes? Getting little kids to do their dirty work for them? It's shameful!'

'We're nothing to do with the Snakes!' said Caro. '*Please* believe us!' she clasped her hands together just like she had when she'd pleaded with Emerald Standing to let her stay at the pub, and looked at Lord and Lady Dockitt beseechingly.

'Just show them the painting, Caro ...' urged Horace.

'I'm trying to!' said Caro. The painting seemed to have got wedged into the pocket and—

'Present arms!' said Lord Dockitt. He sounded like some sort of army general.

They all stared at him. What on earth did he mean?

'You heard him. Show us your wrists,' said Lady Dockitt. 'Go on, stick them out.'

'Why?' asked Horace, instinctively tucking his hands safely inside his coat sleeves.

Lady Dockitt's finger hovered over the silver button again. 'Five, four, three, two—'

'Oh, all right then!'

Caro rolled up her sleeves and stuck her arms out

even though she didn't have a clue why she was being asked to. Horace and Albie followed suit.

'All clear, Doreen?' asked Lord Dockitt as Lady Dockitt inspected their wrists, including one of His Nibs's paws.

'All clear Roly.'

'All clear of what?' asked Caro.

'No snake tattoos visible on any of the suspects' wrists.'

'Snake tattoos?' echoed Albie.

'The police told us,' explained Lord Dockitt with quite a deal of patience, 'that the Snakes are identifiable by the snake tattoos on their wrists.'

How sinister, thought Caro with a prickle of fear.

'So, do you believe us now?' burst out Albie.

'No need for raised voices,' said Lord Dockitt mildly. 'You'll scare the neighbours.'

'Sorry,' said Horace, trying to smooth things over. 'About breaking into your car and hooting the horn and everything, it's just … we really are friends, not foes.'

Finally Caro succeeded in tugging the newspaper-wrapped painting out of the inner pocket of the cape.

'What he means is, all we want to do is return this. Not cause any trouble. Can you just take it and let us go?'

She thought about Ronnie relying on her not to rock the boat.

Well, she'd rocked it big time now.

'Return what?' asked Lord Dockitt. He stepped closer and peered at the package in Caro's hands.

'Your painting,' said Caro. 'The one that belongs up there.'

Lord Dockitt looked up at the gap on the wall and then back at Caro in surprise.

'Well, why didn't you say that in the first place?' cried Lady Dockitt.

'Let me get this clear,' said Lord Dockitt. He was rocking up and down on his heels, just like the policeman in the TV show that Gam liked to watch, *Dixon of Dock Green*. 'Even though it appears you are nothing to do with the Snakes. You stole our painting while we were away ... and now you want to put it back? How peculiar!'

'*Most* peculiar,' agreed Lady Dockitt.

'But we didn't steal it,' said Horace. He looked worried. Very worried. Caro tried to shoot him a reassuring look, although that was the last thing she felt. It was her idea to come here. He hadn't been keen. And now ... would he be arrested too? And Albie? And it would all be her fault.

'Should we listen to what they've got to say, Roly?' asked Lady Dockitt.

'Perhaps we should,' said Lord Dockitt. 'Hand it over then, and follow me into the kitchen. A snack of some sort or another might help, and then we'll see if we can sort this out.'

* * *

In the kitchen, Lord Dockitt bustled about, turning on the grill, slicing a loaf of bread and opening several cans of sardines. It wasn't until they each had a plate crammed with two slices of toast (one white, one brown) topped with four sardines (Lady Dockitt's smothered in bright yellow salad cream) and His Nibs had set to work on a carrot, that Lord Dockitt spoke.

'It's not often,' he said, 'that you get folks doing a good deed. Usually it's the other way round.'

'My thoughts entirely, Roly,' said Lady Dockitt. 'Very well put.'

He picked up the package that Caro had handed over and peeled the newspaper wrapping away. But when the painting revealed itself, instead of looking relieved to have it back, he seemed rather puzzled.

'Well, I never!' he said.

'What, Roly?' enquired Lady Dockitt.

'What's the matter? Aren't you pleased?' asked Caro. He was examining the painting in exactly the same way Horace had earlier, holding it close, then far away, and squinting.

'Sorry to disappoint you,' said Lord Dockitt when he had finally finished his inspection. 'Coming all this way, breaking in using nothing but your bare hands etcetera. But this painting is not, and never has been, ours.'

Chapter Twelve

'What do you mean it's not yours?' said Caro, hurriedly swallowing down the last mouthful of toast and sardines before she completely lost her appetite again. 'It was in the paper. Bird painting by Cornelius ...' The sentence trailed away to nothing. She couldn't remember the artist's full name.

'Cor*nelis* van Pieter,' said Lord Dockitt helpfully.

'Possibly stolen by the Snakes,' offered Horace.

'An *elusive* gang,' added Albie.

'All correct,' said Lord Dockitt. 'But it's not this painting.'

'Ours is *The Skylark*,' said Lady Dockitt.

'And if I'm not mistaken, this is *The Thrush*,' said Lord Dockitt.

'See the speckly bits and the white tips on its wings?' said Lady Dockitt.

A nugget of anxiety lodged itself deep inside Caro's chest. She had thought it would be so easy to return the painting. Case closed. Life could continue as normal.

The spectre of Tom and the Snakes would disappear.

'So you're saying there's more than one of these...' said Horace, his eyes blinking rapidly behind his glasses.

'There are indeed,' said Lord Dockitt. 'Our painting – *The Skylark*, which was stolen while we were on holiday—'

'In the Caribbean,' added Lady Dockitt.

'Oh!' said Horace and he glanced at Lady Dockitt, his eyes lighting up.

'—is one of three,' said Lord Dockitt, ignoring his wife's interruption and Horace's interest. 'All by van Pieter. Collectively known as The Songbirds. *The Skylark*, *The Thrush* and *The Nightingale*. When they are lined up, they all fit together.'

'It's called a triptych,' explained Lady Dockitt. And to Horace, 'It was *ever* so nice, darling. Trinidad, Tobago, St Lucia, Barbados...'

'That's where we're from,' said Horace. 'Barbados.'

Lord Dockitt set the painting down on the table and gave Horace his full attention.

'Barbados is a very fine place,' he said. 'I hope this country is treating you and your parents well. It can't always have been easy.'

'Not always,' said Horace. Because that was the truth.

'I'm sorry about that,' said Lord Dockitt. 'Ignorance usually. Not an excuse though.'

He paused and then shifted his attention back to the painting. '*The Thrush*. It's quite the find. It's been missing for decades, you see. Bit of a mystery in the art world, in fact. Can't remember who originally owned it, but it's believed to have been circulating on the black market for some time.'

'The black market!' echoed Albie. 'What's that?!'

'Illegal trade,' explained Lord Dockitt gravely. 'The selling of stolen goods.'

'And what about the other one? The third painting?' asked Horace.

'*The Nightingale*,' said Lord Dockitt, 'is hanging in the National Gallery. But what I want to know,' he gave Caro a piercing look, 'is how this one came into your possession?'

She'd known the question was coming.

'Uh . . . I . . .' she hesitated.

The painting had been in Jacinta's suitcase. The suitcase had been in Ronnie's cellar. It didn't sound good.

'You'll have to tell them, Caro,' urged Horace. 'We can't get into any more trouble than we already are.'

He was right, of course.

Caro took a deep breath. 'The thing is, I found it in my mum's suitcase ...' she started.

'Well, where *is* your mother?' interrupted Lady Dockitt. 'Does she *know* you're here? We'd better telephone her, hadn't we, Roly, and then she can explain!'

'You can't,' said Caro. 'She can't.'

'Why ever not?'

'Because she's away ...'

'On holiday?'

'On her whistling tour ...'

'A whistling tour?' said Lady Dockitt, suddenly alert. 'Did you hear that, Roly?' She leaned towards Caro. 'I think you'd better tell us your name.'

'Caro Monday,' said Caro. She'd practically told them everything now. What difference would it make giving her name?

Lady Dockitt's eyes blazed. She leapt to her feet, seemingly unable to contain her excitement.

'Do you mean to say your mother is *Jacinta* Monday?!'

she burst out, clasping her hands to her chest in rapture. 'Come to think of it, you *do* look rather similar. Remember, Roly? The lady whistler? The one who performed last year, at the Paris Opera! She was sublime!'

'Yes, dear,' said Lord Dockitt, regarding his wife fondly. 'I do remember, and of course, that is *very* interesting. But, nevertheless …' He turned his attention back to Caro. He wasn't to be so easily deflected. 'I wonder, how did your mother come to have it? How did the painting end up in her suitcase?'

'I don't know,' admitted Caro. 'But I'm sure she'd never steal anything.'

Was she sure?

'She wouldn't,' said Horace stoutly. 'And I've known Caro's mum since I was three.'

'And if you go and tell the police,' piped up Albie, 'Caro says they'll think she *did* steal it!'

Caro watched the Dockitts exchange looks. Lady Dockitt's look was especially intense. They seemed to be having some sort of silent communication.

'We won't tell the police just yet, will we, Roland?' said Lady Dockitt at last. She said it in such a way that there could be no arguing about it.

'It's all highly irregular,' ventured Lord Dockitt. He rose to his feet and began to collect everyone's plates.

'That's as maybe,' said Lady Dockitt. 'But this *is* Jacinta Monday's child we're talking about.'

'Exactly!' said Horace.

They all watched as Lord Dockitt carefully scraped the remains of the meal into the bin and set about piling the dirty crockery into the sink.

'Hide it,' said Lady Dockitt firmly, picking up the painting and handing it back to Caro. 'Keep it safe.'

'Doreen . . .' said Lord Dockitt warningly.

'Let's give the kid a chance, Roly. Or at least wait until her mum comes home. Then they can sort it out together, can't they?' She dazzled him with a smile and threw a wink at Caro. Clearly she was used to getting her own way.

'Thank you,' whispered Caro to Lady Dockitt.

'Very well, then,' said Lord Dockitt reluctantly. 'When will Mrs Monday be back, do you think?'

'Soon,' said Caro, hopefully.

'Ever so soon!' said Horace firmly.

'So soon you wouldn't believe it,' added Albie for good measure.

'Well then, we shall invite her to one of our parties, shan't we, Roly?' said Lady Dockitt. 'Maybe even throw one in her honour.'

'Hmmm,' said Lord Dockitt. He left the sink and

came back to sit at the table. He put his hands together and closed his eyes. When he opened them again, he met Caro's very serious gaze with an even more solemn one of his own.

'It'd be my guess that whoever stole our painting will want yours, too. So, keep your eyes and ears open. If you feel in the slightest danger, you must come back AT ONCE, and then we'll *have* to get the police involved. Understood?'

Caro nodded. Best not to tell Lord Dockitt about the phone call. Or the intruder. If she did, he might change his mind.

Carefully, Caro put the painting back inside the pocket in her cape. And as she did, she noticed that even though – in reality – it was very light, by some strange alchemy it suddenly felt very, very heavy. Weighted down with ... what? Fear? Uncertainty? A very large dollop of mystery.

They'd come to the Dockitts' to get rid of the painting. But instead, here she was still stuck with it, along with a whole lot of extra complications.

Was Mum involved? Was Tom a Snake? Did that mean he was going to come after her?

Were the Snakes out to get her already?

As they set off in the direction of home, Caro

thought about what Lady Dockitt had said and decided she was right.

Hide the painting. Keep it safe.

Just until Jacinta and Ronnie came home.

* * *

By the time they got back to Waterloo, it was almost dawn. The black night sky had thinned to a murky grey, and Big Ben donged five.

In the Rubbles, Caro climbed into the car and hid the painting in the gap between the yellow foam and the red leather. It was the safest place she could think of. No one would know to look there.

As the Underground was closed and Albie was too tired to walk all the way back to Hampstead, it was agreed he could sleep in the car.

Horace showed him how to crank the front seat back as far as it would go to make a sort of bed.

'I'm going to take His Nibs home to the hutch,' announced Caro, 'and while I'm there I'll get you a blanket, Albie.'

'And I need to get home before Mum wakes up,' said Horace.

The two parted ways at Waterloo Road, with Caro

and His Nibs continuing through the snaggle of back streets to the pub. But at her corner they stopped.

The street wasn't empty. A little further down, two hulks hovered either side of the pub's front door. Cautiously, Caro scooped up His Nibs and crept back into the shadows, watching as a trail of cigarette smoke merged into the grey murk of the morning air. A leather jacket. No. *Two* leather jackets. Could it be the men she'd greeted in the pub earlier that evening? The ones with the shiny, rock-hard quiff and that bushy moustache? Why were they still here? Last orders had been hours and hours ago!

'This is odd,' she muttered to her rabbit.

Was Tom in league with them? Might he have sent them to look for her? To get the painting?

Ronnie would say, 'You're jumping to conclusions, Caro.'

But what if she wasn't?

'Bit of a coincidence, isn't it?' she murmured to His Nibs. 'That we've never seen them before tonight?' His Nibs blinked twice in agreement.

Stealthily, Caro hoisted His Nibs over her shoulder, took several steps backwards, and then darted into the alley that led to the backs of the houses. It was the kind of alley that doesn't go anywhere, ending in a steep brick wall, beyond which was the elevated railway track. But just before the wall, there was a gate which led into the back yard of the pub.

The gate creaked as Caro pushed it open. Very quietly she opened the hutch door, popped His Nibs inside and fetched some fresh hay. Then she climbed onto the big dustbin, swung easily up to her bedroom window and crawled inside.

It took less than a minute to grab a spare blanket from the pile on top of the wardrobe, and Caro was just about to climb back out of the window when the sight of her suitcase on her bed made her stop.

That wasn't right. She came back into the room and looked at it thoughtfully. When she'd fetched it up earlier, she hadn't put it on the bed; she'd put it on the floor. She hadn't opened it either. But the buckles were partially unfastened.

She opened the suitcase properly and surveyed the contents. It hadn't been very neatly packed in the first place so it was hard to tell if anything had been disturbed. Sometimes, on the rare occasions they'd taken a holiday (to Brighton for a couple of days last year, to Lake Windermere for a whole week the year before that), Ronnie or Jacinta helped her unpack. Perhaps Mrs Emerald Standing had started to do the same? Or…

A more unwelcome thought.

What if Tom had already followed her? Slipped inside the pub while those leather jackets guarded the door? He'd tried to get the painting before and failed. Then he'd got the job of nanny at Heath View, presumably to have another go. He wasn't going to give up that easily, was he?

She sniffed the air, but all she could detect was a sort of beery smell. It was what all the rooms smelled like in the pub, quite nice when you got used to it. There was none of that lemony leathery scent – but then there wouldn't be, would there? Tom's cologne was in the Rubbles, safely tucked in Albie's rucksack.

In the room next door, Ronnie and Jacinta's room, the bed creaked. Emerald Standing was in there fast asleep. Perhaps Caro should go in there, wake her up and tell her … what? That maybe … possibly … or maybe not … there'd been an intruder?

She had promised not to cause any trouble. To stay out of Mrs Standing's way, to take care of herself.

And what if she was wrong and she *had* put the suitcase on the bed? Oh, *why* was everything such a muddle? Caro yawned. She was so tired she couldn't even think straight. Meanwhile, Albie was all on his own waiting for her, shivering away in the Rubbles.

Quickly, Caro climbed back out of the window, bounced off the dustbin and whispered goodbye to His Nibs. Tonight she'd camp out with Albie in the Rubbles. To be on the safe side, she wouldn't sleep. She hadn't forgotten those two sinister figures outside the pub. She would stay awake and be on guard. Just in case.

Chapter Thirteen

Caro did sleep, of course she did.

'I'm glad you're staying, Caro,' Albie had whispered when she had reappeared and cranked down the car seat next to him, and covered them both with the blanket. Albie was brave, but not that brave. He hadn't been looking forward to being all alone in the Rubbles, even if it was almost morning.

'You're welcome,' Caro had mumbled.

Then they had plunged into a deep sleep, and continued to sleep as the sun rose, casting long blades of light across the wasteland; as, in the distance, the hum of traffic grew; as all over London people hurried to work, to offices, and hospitals, to garages and depots, to small shops and large department stores.

Across the river, busy with boats and barges, Big Ben marked time: six, seven, eight, nine, ten.

It wasn't until noon that Horace arrived and forced them out of their slumber.

'Wake up, sleepyheads!' he crowed, opening all the car's doors so that gusts of fresh air burst in, making them sit up and blink like startled rabbits.

Rabbits! thought Caro in a panicky rush. His Nibs, all alone and breakfast-less.

'I have to go and feed His Nibs,' she said as she flung the blanket to one side. 'Wait for me, I'll be back soon.'

* * *

'I need to talk to you,' said Toby as soon as Caro dashed into the pub. The place was in full swing, as it always was at lunchtime: the regulars chatting and supping their pints; the plates of hot sausage rolls and steaming meat pies jostling for space on the counter. Caro would've given anything to see Ronnie bustling behind the bar, or for Jacinta to suddenly appear whistling one of her tunes. But instead, here was Toby blocking her path, his quiff flatter than ever, looking quite frantic.

'Not now,' said Caro. Whatever it was, it would have to wait. There was no time to chat. She just wanted to get His Nibs and go back to the Rubbles. And ... an insistent thought niggled away. Was it really enough just to lie low and keep the painting hidden?

She elbowed Toby out of the way and headed into the kitchen.

'*You* were up early this morning.'

It was Mrs Emerald Standing, leaning against the kitchen sink puffing on a long thin cigarillo. She raised an elegant eyebrow and tipped a quantity of ash into Ronnie's favourite gold-rimmed teacup.

'Yes,' said Caro. Why did that matter? Hadn't Mrs Standing said she could only stay if she looked after herself?

'Toby,' said Emerald sharply, looking past Caro. 'Stop loitering and get back to work.'

She wasn't very motherly, thought Caro, as Toby reluctantly turned and skulked back into the bar. She always seemed to be annoyed with him about one thing or another.

Mind you, Caro and Ronnie had always been annoyed with him too.

Outside, she opened the hutch and His Nibs bounded out joyfully.

'Want to come to the Rubbles for a bit?' she asked. He twitched his nose – *yes* – and Caro looked about for the pram so that she could return it to Horace. It wasn't there.

'Where's the pram?' she shouted. But there was no reply, and when she peered in at the door, the kitchen was empty.

'We'll have to get it later then,' she said to the rabbit. 'Come on. I saw a nice patch of dandelions in the Rubbles for your breakfast.'

Back in the saloon the radio was blaring: *'No one knows who heads up the Snakes, say Scotland Yard. The shadowy gang who hide behind—'*

'Caro, I need to . . .' said Toby, clicking off the radio. Good. She didn't want to hear anything more about the Snakes. They gave her the creeps. Everywhere she went, they seemed to follow her around.

Someone tugged at Caro's arm. She stopped listening to Toby and spun round.

'Caro, a chap was in here looking for you earlier.' The speaker was one of the regulars. Pete was his name.

'Red-haired fella,' continued Pete. 'Said it was important. Said to tell you he's in the café down the road.'

Red-haired fella? Caro felt a thump of dread.

So Tom *had* followed her. Or perhaps he had followed Albie. She gathered up His Nibs and hugged him to her.

'Friendly chap,' said Pete.

Friendly! Pete didn't know the half of it. That cheerful look of Tom's was a grotesque mask, thought Caro. He'd been in the pub charming the locals and... Her thoughts whipped back to last night and the suitcase on her bed, and the odd feeling she'd had: not sure if someone had moved it, or opened it, or rifled through it. And now he was *waiting* for her in the café down the road.

Did he think she was stupid? Did he think she hadn't already guessed who he really was?

'Caro!' said Toby. He was still hovering, his mouth opening and closing like a fish.

'Which café?' she asked Pete, ignoring Toby. 'Steady Eddie's?' It was where Jacinta took her for pie and mash, washed down with giant mugs of bright orange tea.

'Nope. He wanted coffee, so I told him Joe's,' said Pete.

* * *

Like all the locals, Pete called it Joe's but really it was Gio's, an Italian café on the corner of The Cut.

Caro peered in through the window, past the chrome machine that sizzled and steamed and spurted out coffee and frothy hot chocolate; past the plates piled high with tiny pastries dusted with icing sugar and filled with cinnamon and nuts and a sort of custard cream. She scanned the booths and the tall swivel stools at the bar. His Nibs stayed close by her ankles. She didn't blame him.

'He's there,' she whispered. Tucked into the corner booth; face buried in a newspaper, tiny cup of coffee by his side. From behind the glass, Giovanni waved and pointed at a pastry. Caro mouthed, 'Later,' and sprang away from the window before Tom could turn round.

She and His Nibs ran the whole way to the Rubbles. Horace was helping Albie hoist his rucksack onto his back.

'I'm just going,' said Albie. 'Horace is coming part of the way with me ... Caro, what's the matter?'

'Tom's here,' she gasped. She leaned into the car. In its hiding place, a corner of the painting was clearly visible. She shoved it further into the gap between the red leather and the yellow foam. 'He's in Gio's. Cool as a cucumber, reading the paper and drinking one of those tiny cups of coffee.'

'Espresso,' said Horace knowledgeably. 'I prefer cappuccino but Aunty Sandra—'

'Horace!' Caro snapped. 'Forget about espresso. Did you just hear what I said? TOM is here.'

Behind his glasses, Horace's eyes blinked just like His Nibs's did when he was startled.

'Sorry!' cried Caro. The last thing she wanted to do was hurt her friend. But this was important. 'What are we going to do?' Her heart was hammering nineteen to the dozen.

'You're panicking,' said Horace. 'Take deep breaths, Caro.'

She *was* panicking. She was a panicker, Ronnie always said that. She took a big gulp of air and then another. Horace picked up His Nibs and put him into her arms.

'I *can't* . . .' she said. 'Because . . .'

Because she was out of her depth. Because she had run out of ideas. Because . . .

Albie was oblivious to the panic. He gave an excited little jump.

'But it's all right, don't you see? This is our chance!' he said, shrugging off his rucksack and chucking it to the ground.

'Chance to do what?' asked Caro. Horace was

looking straight at her. He put a steadying hand on her shoulder and breathed with her. In, out, in out.

'Just ask him!'

Albie looked positively excited. Acting like he was in the middle of some kind of adventure story. Meanwhile Caro's heart was pounding like it had gone into overdrive.

'Ask him *what*?'

'I think he means,' said Horace, 'if Tom's here then why don't we seize the moment. Corner him. Ask all the questions. What's that saying? Know your enemy.'

Know your enemy. That sounded good. It sounded in control and it made Caro feel better. She rested her cheek on the rabbit's forehead. *Cou-rage*, Victor would say.

'All right,' she said. She *did* need to find out exactly what Tom was up to. She couldn't run for ever. She had to take action. Now.

'We could catch him,' said Horace.

'And when we've caught him, we can make him confess,' said Albie.

'Find out why the painting was in your suitcase in the first place ...' said Horace

'And *then* we can go to the police,' said Caro.

There was a short silence while they all felt extremely pleased with themselves.

'But *how* will we catch him?' asked Horace.

'A trap!' Albie jumped up. 'I saw it earlier when I was exploring—'

'Saw what?' asked Caro.

'A hole, a big one over there.' Albie pointed a little way off to a part of the Rubbles they used for building stuff out of planks of wood. There were a couple of ramshackle dens made of old blackboards banged together with rusty nails. And to one side, a crater. No one knew who had dug it. It had been there for ever, since they had first come to the Rubbles.

'Edwin fell in it. D'you remember Caro?' said Horace.

She did. He had cried blue murder. Been covered in bruises. Mrs Braithwaite had said they weren't to take him anywhere near the Rubbles until he was at least seven.

'We can fix it so Tom falls into it,' said Albie. 'Cover it up, disguise it with twigs and leaves and stuff.'

'And those bamboo sticks we got from the allotments!' said Horace.

'All we have to do is lure him in,' continued Albie, his eyes alight. 'And then . . .'

'Gotcha!' cried Caro, releasing His Nibs and sticking her fist in the air.

They dragged the bamboo sticks in place, taking care to scatter them wider than the circumference of the hole so that they became part of the landscape. They filled in any tell-tale gaps with twigs and clumps of weeds and mud.

They agreed that Albie was the fastest runner, and Caro drew a map on a scrap of paper so that he could find his way to Gio's. They decided that he would stand outside the café and wave, and then, when Tom saw him, he was to run like billy-o, keeping just enough ahead that Tom could follow but not catch up.

Caro and Horace and His Nibs positioned themselves on the other side of the hole, watching as Albie disappeared through the gap in the fence.

'Will it work?' she asked anxiously. If Tom really was a Snake, might he be too clever for them?

'If it all goes wrong ...' started Horace. He was as nervous as she was.

'It can't,' she said, trying to convince herself as much as him, and then Albie was back, his stick-like legs running for all they were worth, and here was Tom, close on his heels dashing across the Rubbles, skirting the tyre swings, weaving amongst the blackboard dens, veering past the car. At the last minute, Albie sidestepped the hidden hole and joined his friends.

'Tom!' yelled Caro, waving.

Tom stopped and waved back enthusiastically, and then he was running again, closer, closer, and... at just the right moment, Caro stepped back from the hole and Tom lurched into nothingness and disappeared in a great cacophony of bamboo and mud and twig.

Caro was so relieved the plan had worked that she started to shriek with hysterical laughter.

No one noticed that Horace had gone completely quiet.

He ran to the hole and peered over the side; then he jerked back up, his face stricken.

'Caro!' he said. 'That isn't your nanny person. That's Tomaz Topaz! The acrobat I told you about. From the circus!'

Chapter Fourteen

Caro stared at Horace. Apart from the distant rumble of traffic on Waterloo Road and the intermittent cry of the rag-and-bone man making his way along Coin Street, it was deathly quiet.

'What are you talking about?' she said.

'You must remember! When I went to the circus! The day you found out you had to go to Hampstead. I *told* you. About his outfit and everything.'

Caro did remember. Turquoise sequins. Death-defying feats on the tightrope.

She'd been desperate to know all about the acrobat's balancing techniques. Little had she known then how soon she'd get the opportunity to observe Mr Topaz right up close.

She dropped down next to Horace and stuck her head over the edge of the hole. Albie and His Nibs did the same.

Tom/Tomaz was staring up at them furiously, spluttering and coughing and trying to bat bits of twig and mud out of his face and eyes and hair.

It was an extremely large, deep hole. There was no chance of him getting out on his own. From this angle, he wasn't even remotely threatening. He actually looked rather small.

Caro had never seen Tom/Tomaz look cross before. He had always been jolly, forever smiling and laughing. Now his face was almost as red as his hair.

The mask had come off.

'Caro Monday,' he said, somehow knowing she was the ringleader. 'Did you do this on purpose? I could've broken a bone!'

'Did you?' asked Caro heartlessly.

He felt his wrists and ankles gingerly. 'Well, no, as it happens. And there's no need to sound so antagonising. I *might* have sprained something. And in my line of work that just won't do.' He winced, closed his eyes and then opened them again, as though by some miracle he might wake up from a bad dream.

'Well then, stop complaining,' said Caro. She felt braver now he was trapped inside the hole. A snake in his pit. She couldn't believe they'd been taken in by him for all that time.

'Honestly,' he continued, 'I try to do someone a favour and this is the thanks I get.'

'Do who a favour?' asked Horace suspiciously.

'And who, may I ask, are you?' said Tom.

'You know Horace ...' started Caro. And then she realised that Tom *hadn't* met Horace. He had always been reading on his bench on Parliament Hill when she and Albie and Horace had met in the Wilds to build the gym.

'This is Horace and you'd better be nice to him,' she said.

'Caro!' said Tom. 'What's got into you? When have you known me not be nice to anyone?'

'Do who a favour?' repeated Horace. They weren't going to let Tom dodge any of the questions.

'Marks, of course. She asked me to come and fetch Albie back. *And* you, Caro. We can work something out about the rabbit! It's not worth running away for.'

'Liar,' said Caro. Was he lying? His story sounded quite genuine.

But how *could* it be?

'What?' said Tom, looking shocked. 'Look, what's all this about? Can you at least give me a hand out so we can talk sensibly?'

'No,' said Albie. 'You're staying in there until we get some answers.'

'Until you confess,' said Caro.

'Confess to what?' Tom looked genuinely flabbergasted. A nugget of doubt began to work its way into Caro's mind. Now he was here in front of her, it was hard to believe that he was in with a gang as dangerous as the Snakes.

'Well, for a start you can tell us who you really are,' said Horace. 'You just said that if you'd sprained something it wouldn't help in *your line of work*. What does that mean?'

'Just admit it!' said Caro, making a big effort to ignore the doubts. 'Are you Tom the nanny or Tomaz Topaz the acrobat – as seen by Horace at the circus? When was that, Horace?'

'Not last Sunday but the Sunday before that,' said Horace.

'Oh, that!' said Tom and at last his face seemed to clear. 'That's easy to explain. You don't need to be so worked up about it.'

'Just start talking!' said Caro. She didn't like being

told not to get worked up about *anything*. Nobody did. 'Are you a nanny or an acrobat? What were you doing in my room? Little did you know, your *cologne* gave you away...'

Albie dug in his pocket and pulled out the bottle of Russian Leather. Caro snatched it from him. Untwisting the cap, she poured the contents out as dramatically as she was able. The liquid splashed onto the ground and the pungent smell of leather and lemons filled the air.

'Caro, that's evidence!' said Albie. 'Maybe you should've kept it—'

'Evidence of WHAT?' shouted Tom. 'And why have you got my cologne?'

He stopped talking, gave a great bellow of frustration, and then, crouching down and pressing his hands into the ground, like a jack in the box, in one spectacular leap, sprang out of the hole.

They all staggered back in surprise.

'Why are you looking at me like that? I'm not a monster! I'm not going to hurt you,' he cried.

'Aren't you?' said Caro. She moved close to Horace. Albie moved closer to her. He *was* clever! He had superhuman powers! Who could jump out of a hole like that?

'You want the truth? Well, you shall have it – it's not the secret of the century ... I *am* an acrobat. Tomaz Topaz is my stage name. But the circus season has finished. You ...' he nodded at Horace, 'would've seen the last show. But as it happens, we performers need to earn money until we start again for the summer season.'

'Well, why didn't you say!' burst out Caro, forgetting about the interrogation for a minute. 'You know my ambitions. All that time we were going for walks on the heath you could have been teaching me your acrobatic skills!'

'Do you think your great-aunt would've given me the job if I'd advertised my profession?' retorted Tom. 'No. She wouldn't. Some people don't approve of circus folk. I thought it best to keep it quiet.'

Tom stopped to draw breath. 'Now,' he started again, as though he was a teacher summoning all his strength to deal with an uncooperative class. 'Do you want me to tell my story or not?'

'I suppose so,' said Caro grudgingly. It was very hard not to believe the words coming out of the red-faced person in front of them.

'I saw an advert in the newsagent's and when I realised it was Billy's house—'

'*Who?*' interrupted Caro.

'You *must* know about Billy,' said Tom, raking his hands through his hair.

'No. We don't. Is he something to do with Gam?' asked Caro.

'Of *course* he's to do with your great-aunt,' said Tom. 'He was her son!'

Chapter Fifteen

Caro sat down on the ground with a thump. His Nibs stopped munching on a small clump of borage. Albie and Horace looked at each other, eyes wide.

Gam had a son? What was Tom talking about? There was no sign there'd ever been a *son* in the house... there were no old photographs, no children's things... unless... now Caro remembered the shelf of children's books in Tom's bedroom.

'Mum never said anything...' Caro started. This son, she suddenly realised, would've been Jacinta's cousin.

'We were friends years ago, before the war,' said Tom, sitting down on an old tyre so that he was opposite

Caro. Albie and Horace stayed standing, like guards. Just in case.

'He was the only one who played with me.' A cloud seemed to pass across Tom's features.

'Why wouldn't anyone else play with you?' asked Horace.

'I lived in a children's home. Most of the other kids avoided us like the plague. And if they weren't avoiding us, they were tormenting us. We weren't like them, see.'

Horace nodded. He did see. All his life he had been different. Even though he'd come to this country when he was a tiny baby – even though thousands of Caribbean folk worked on the trains and the buses, in the hospitals and for the postal service – certain people still thought he didn't belong. But he *did* belong. Just like Tom had.

'Billy saw me for who I was,' Tom was saying. 'Not just as a kid whose parents had abandoned him. His whole family were kind, and welcoming and... happy,' said Tom wistfully. 'I used to imagine what it would be like growing up in a family like that.'

Caro wondered where all this was leading. It didn't seem to have anything to do with why Tom wanted the painting. *Or* explain his involvement with the Snakes.

'But everything changed with the war,' sighed Tom.

'The entire children's home was evacuated. I was sent to stay with a family up north, near Leeds. Wasn't happy. Ran away to join the circus and didn't find out that Billy had died in the Blitz until years later. And now,' he shrugged helplessly, 'Well ... I wanted to tell Mary how sorry I was. But when I arrived, she didn't recognise me, and then I missed the moment. And now it's too late to explain.'

'So, let me get this straight,' said Caro, crossing her arms, 'Gam had a son, and he's dead? But if that's true, how can she hate children so much?'

'Is that what you think? That your great-aunt hates you? Caro, she really doesn't. I think she's just scared of getting close to anyone after what happened.'

'But why didn't Mum *tell* me she had this cousin. Why would she keep it a secret?'

'Maybe she didn't mean to keep it a secret,' said Tom. He was looking at her very seriously, giving her his full attention. 'Maybe it's just that some things are too painful to talk about.'

Caro thought about that for a minute. She supposed it made sense. Big things, scary things, could sometimes be hard to put into words. They were hard to even *think* about without getting sucked in. Like her nightmare that Jacinta might never come back.

Or that other thing about Caro and mum and Ronnie not being a family any more.

'You knew her, then? My mum?' she asked. Momentarily, she forgot about the Snakes, and the painting, and Tom's interest in it.

'Of course I did. She and Billy were always together. You didn't get one without the other,' said Tom. 'I knew Mr Monday, too.'

'Mr Monday?' asked Caro. Tom was full of surprises today.

'Oh yeah! Remember, Caro,' said Albie. 'When the policeman came? Mrs Monday said something about still having her wedding ring.'

Oh yes. In all the excitement, that revelation had been forgotten.

'He was a wonderful chap,' said Tom and his eyes seemed to go all misty and far away. 'Worked as a foreign correspondent, so he wasn't about much, travelling here, there and everywhere; but when he was at home, he was brilliant, always building something out of nothing, and always whistling. He could whistle anything. And they whistled together, all three of them. Mary pretended it drove her mad, but she loved it really.'

Caro couldn't imagine Great Aunt Mary loving *anything*.

'She's changed, Mary,' said Tom, as if he had guessed Caro's thoughts. 'That happens when you lose people.'

'What happened to Mr Monday?' asked Caro.

'Don't know. I assume he died in the war like Billy. He would've been sent somewhere to do his reporting and...' Tom trailed off.

'That's sad,' said Albie, and Horace nodded so emphatically his glasses nearly fell off.

They were right, thought Caro. It was sad. Imagine your child dying and your husband dying and then... and then Jacinta running away.

But Jacinta had *had* to run away because Gam had been so horrible!

There was so much to understand. Even if Tom was right and some things *were* too painful to talk about, it was odd that Jacinta had never – not even once – mentioned her cousin or her uncle.

'I wanted to tell Mary who I am,' Tom continued. 'And I suppose I do look quite different to the scrawny lad I was back then. But Marks said I should leave it, and that anything to do with the past upsets Mary something rotten. *That's* why she was so upset about the rabbit.'

'What do you mean?'

'Billy had a rabbit.' Tom looked over at His Nibs who

had moved on from the clump of borage to a patch of dandelion leaves. 'I suppose he reminded her of him.'

'Oh,' said Caro. Her hand crept into her pocket and she felt for the little rabbit book she'd taken from Tom's room the day before.

Billy's property, then.

'So anyway,' Tom said, 'that's the history lesson over. I still don't get what this has to do with my cologne.'

Tom had taken Caro by surprise with his fantastical story, but she wasn't ready to be fobbed off just yet.

She kicked the ground where the cologne had collected in a puddle and a whiff of lemons and leather rose up again.

'Someone was in my room, someone who smelled of ... this ... and honestly, the only person it could be in the whole wide world is you. *You* were the intruder. And you want the painting, don't you?'

'What painting?' asked Tom, the picture of innocence.

'Don't say you don't know!' scoffed Caro.

'Caro,' said Horace. 'Maybe he really doesn't ...'

'You're on his side now, are you?' she said. Although she had to admit that Tom really didn't seem to have a clue.

'This is all news to me,' said Tom. 'I didn't sneak

into your room. And I don't know anything about a painting. I think *you* owe *me* an explanation.'

'But the cologne...'

'For goodness' sake!' exploded Tom. 'I'm not the only one who wears a two-shillings-and-sixpence cologne from Woolworths. I wouldn't be surprised if every young lad between sixteen and twenty-nine has a bottle. Someone may've been in your room that night, in fact, they were – Mrs Monday told me about the break-in – but it wasn't me. Let's go to the police now if you'd like that cleared up once and for all!'

Caro was aware that Albie and Horace were watching her. Waiting for her to take the lead. But she could already see that they believed him.

'Show me your wrists,' she said.

'What?'

'Show me.'

Tom held out his wrists. Both bare. No sign of any tattoo.

'I think he's telling the truth, Caro. He can't be anything to do with the Snakes,' said Horace quietly.

He was right, thought Caro. Tom hadn't acted remotely guilty. He wasn't remotely scary either. And the Snakes *were* scary. They chopped off people's fingers and sent them in the post.

In her heart of hearts, Caro knew Tom wasn't capable of that.

'You think I'm a Snake! That gang?' Tom laughed. 'You kids! Your imaginations really have got the better of you this time!' He looked at them fondly, like they were just playing a game. 'Look. I'm here because Marks sent me to get you. She's petrified about how upset Mary will be when she finds out you've gone.'

'She'll be all right without me,' said Caro.

'You're wrong there,' said Tom. 'Think about it, Caro. She lost Billy. Then your mother ran away and then ...'

'Because of the way Gam treated her!' Caro burst out. What did he know about Jacinta? Nothing!

But even as the words left her mouth, she realised there was so much she didn't know. And didn't Ronnie always say there were two sides to every story?

'Marks doesn't know why,' said Tom, 'but when Mary came home yesterday after the rabbit incident, she was in a terrible state.'

'Because of her bad back,' said Albie.

'That's what we thought at first,' said Tom. 'But Marks wasn't sure. Something seemed to have upset her a great deal.'

'She was probably still hysterical about His Nibs,' cut in Caro.

'Marks didn't think it *was* that. But Mary insists it's her back and you know how stubborn she is.'

They did.

'You *can't* run away,' pleaded Tom. 'Marks is adamant I mustn't come back without you.'

But going back would be like knowingly taking His Nibs to the gallows, thought Caro. 'Gam telephoned the RSPCA!' she said. 'She hasn't changed her mind about that has she?'

'Not in so many words...' said Tom honestly.

'I'll come,' said Albie. He stood up and placed his hand in Tom's. He liked Tom. He really liked Marks, and he had even started to like Gam a little bit recently.

And he couldn't live in the car in the Rubbles for ever, could he?

'Well, one's better than none. And I suppose it might help to keep the peace for now,' said Tom. 'Have they said it's all right for you to stay at the pub?' he asked Caro.

'Yes, Mrs Standing says it's fine,' she said.

'Well, I don't know... Mrs Monday won't be happy. And nor will Marks. And what about your Ronnie? Perhaps I should come and talk to this Mrs Standing myself, just to be sure.'

Mrs Standing had told Caro she could stay if she

took care of herself. But if Tom turned up asking if everything was all right ... well it would muddy the waters, and ... She couldn't risk it.

'You ran away,' she blurted out. 'To the circus. And you've turned out all right, haven't you? And besides, this is my home!'

The truth was, a tiny part of Caro would have quite liked to go back to Hampstead. It might feel safer there with Tom and Marks ... but she couldn't go, could she? She had to be here when Jacinta got back. Guard the painting. Look after His Nibs.

Tom looked at her long and hard.

'Well, all right then,' he said. 'Now you've put it that way. But you *must* promise to come back if anything goes wrong.'

* * *

'Shouldn't you have explained properly about the painting, Caro?' asked Horace after Albie and Tom had set off in the direction of the tube.

'He seemed to think it was all a game,' she said. 'And what if I had? Then he'd *definitely* have got all worried and made me go back with them. Or stuck his oar in before we've had a chance to prove Mum's innocence—'

Caro stopped talking.

'Uh-oh,' she said.

A little further down the street the Bully Boys had emerged from the sweet shop. Bother. She didn't feel like fighting now. Plus, neither of them had any ammunition.

She grabbed Horace's elbow and steered him across the road and into a doorway, so they were out of sight. Obediently, His Nibs followed.

'Look,' said Horace. She followed his gaze. Two figures were approaching the Bully Boys. Two figures dressed in black leather jackets. Them again! The same men who had been hanging around the pub. The one with the shiny rock-hard quiff and the other one with the bushy moustache. How did *they* know the Bully Boys?

'D'you think *they're* the Snakes?' whispered Caro. And if they were, did that mean the Bully Boys were involved too?

From their hiding place, Caro and Horace watched a conversation taking place, the leather jackets talking intently, the Bully Boys shaking their heads and shrinking back. The leather jackets leaned in, jutting their necks forward in a threatening manner.

'Do you think they're all right?' asked Horace.

'Good riddance!' said Caro unsympathetically. 'Let them see what it's like to be bullied for a change.' But really, she was just relieved the sinister men weren't talking to her and Horace like that.

'Yes, but...' said Horace.

The leather jackets were right up close to the Bully Boys now. One of them held up a piece of paper, waved it about, and shoved it into the pocket of the one called Stanley.

Then they swaggered away.

'I wonder what that was all about?' said Horace.

'I don't know,' admitted Caro. Were the men Snakes? Did they know about her and the painting? Or was she just putting two and two together to make six just like she had with Tom.

'If it wasn't Tom in my room in Hampstead,' she said, 'then who was it?'

'It doesn't matter now,' said Horace patiently.

'Doesn't matter?' echoed Caro. 'It does, doesn't it, His Nibs?' How could Horace think that? Of course it mattered!

'Well, whoever was in your room in Hampstead *hasn't* followed you here, have they?' said Horace. 'Or telephoned you again. So, they *can't* know you're back in the pub.'

Perhaps Horace was right. She had no proof that those men were Snakes. It was a hunch. An unproven hunch. And anyway, the truth was, they hadn't shown the slightest bit of interest in her when she'd been in the pub.

Still, what about last night? That odd feeling that someone *had* been in her room. Rooting around in her case.

'All you have to do is lie low until your mum comes home,' said Horace confidently. 'The painting is safe. No one will find it. And then when she gets back, it'll all be sorted out. I bet there'll be a simple explanation.'

'I hope so,' said Caro dubiously. It was all right for Horace to act so calm and collected. *He* hadn't seen the figure in the mirror at Hampstead. *He* hadn't been frightened out of his wits. And, besides, he seemed to be forgetting that the theft of the Dockitts' painting was real.

Because it *was* real. And the Snakes were real too.

And it was scary.

Chapter Sixteen

Back in the pub, the phone was ringing.

'Caro, it's for you,' shouted Toby. 'And when you're finished, I need to—'

Caro took the phone and His Nibs bounded towards the kitchen and out into the back yard.

'Thank goodness! You're safe!' It was Ronnie, her voice tight with worry.

'Of course I'm safe ...' started Caro, but Ronnie spoke over her.

'I just rang Hampstead because I wanted to give you some news about your mum – and thank goodness I did. What are you doing, Caro? Running away like that? Marks says you just left, no warning whatsoever, and the other ward followed you. Is it true?'

'Yes but—'

'Oh Caro! I've got enough on my plate without you adding to my worries!'

Caro could have kicked herself. She should have phoned Ronnie yesterday and now it looked worse than it was.

'I couldn't stay there,' she tried to explain. 'Because of Gam – I mean Great Aunt Mary. She doesn't like rabbits.'

'What?! But, Caro, you weren't meant to *take* the rabbit in the first place! I told you to leave him at the pub!'

There was a silence. Caro twisted the curly pale blue telephone wire around her fingers, stretched it, and let it spring back. She felt bad.

'But I couldn't bear to leave him here,' she said in a small voice. 'I knew I was going to miss you and mum so much ... and then when Gam found out, she went completely mad and called the RSPCA and asked them to come and take him away!'

Ronnie sighed.

'I know it's been difficult for you, Caro. But I'll be home soon.'

'When?' asked Caro eagerly.

She heard a bell tinkle in the background.

'Coming in a minute, Marjorie!' called Ronnie. She was using her 'I'm trying to be patient' voice.

'She's really down,' she said to Caro quietly. 'The op has knocked her for six. But Harry's on his way back now and once he's here, and I've shown him the ropes, I'll be on that train quick as you like. If all goes well I'll be back in a couple of days.'

'OK,' Caro said. Should she tell Ronnie now that she was frightened? That she was out of her depth? If she did, she knew Ronnie would drop everything and come back straight away. But then what about Marjorie? Feeling all down. No. She would have to wait. Two days wasn't long.

'Caro, can you put me on to Mrs Standing, please love? I'll need to square the new arrangement with her.'

'It's OK, I've already squared it,' said Caro. 'She says it's fine. But – what were you going to tell me about Mum?'

There was a pause, and Caro guessed that Ronnie was deliberating about whether she should insist on speaking to Emerald or not. The bell tinkled again. 'I'll have to be quick... I've been talking to the consulate in Manaus... YES, Marjorie, in a MINUTE!'

'And it turns out, instead of flying straight to New York like she was meant to, your mum changed her plans. They think she might have gone to Panama instead...'

Panama? The name rang a bell. Where had Caro heard about that before?

'So we mustn't worry. They're doing everything they can to find her. It's just ... it's taking a bit longer than usual because there's been this attempted coup ...'

'A coup? Like Che Guevara and the Cuban Revolution?' asked Caro. It had been one of the favourite talking points in the pub last year.

'Sort of. There was a plot to seize power,' Ronnie explained. 'But it wasn't successful. And of course it's making it almost impossible to get hold of *any* information. Why on earth she had to go there, I don't know!'

The bell tinkled again quite loud this time and Caro sensed Ronnie's exasperation. 'Coming, Marjorie! You still there, Caro?'

''Course I am!'

'Hopefully we'll hear more soon. I'll telephone as soon as I do. Promise to be good and don't get under Mrs Standing's feet etcetera; OK?'

'Promise,' said Caro. She replaced the receiver

carefully. She felt strangely trembly. Mum couldn't have anything to do with the Snakes if she was caught up in a revolution, could she? Caro missed her and Ronnie so much it hurt. Now a sob lurched up into her throat and out of her mouth.

She went into the yard and lifted His Nibs into his hutch. She gave him some clean hay and some fresh water.

'You all right, love?' asked one of the regulars as she walked back into the saloon.

'Fine thanks,' she said, and clattered up the stairs and into the bathroom. She closed the door behind her and sat on the edge of the bath. Breathe. Stay calm. *At least you know now that Mum is alive,* she told herself. Even if she has gone and got herself into an almighty revolution-type scrape. All that needs to happen now is for the authorities to find her and tell her to come back as quickly as possible. Then you can sort out this mess together.

Caro ran the tap and splashed cold water on her face. Then she opened the bathroom cabinet to find Jacinta's cologne, just to smell it, just to remember, just to feel close to her...

Sitting on the shelf staring straight at her was a bottle of Russian Leather.

What?!

She grabbed the bottle. Unscrewed the lid. Took a sniff.

Leather and lemons. Rushing up her nostrils. Making her feel sick.

Tom had said everyone wore it. That it was only two and sixpence from Woolworths. But this couldn't be just another coincidence, could it?

The only other male in the place was Toby. She'd never noticed him wearing any cologne before. But who else could it belong to?

Could it be him? That galumphing idiot? Had *he* followed her to Hampstead, broken into the house and crept into her room?

Scaring the living daylights out of her?

Scaring Gam too.

Surely not. He wasn't capable!

She crossed into her bedroom, slammed the door shut and leaned against it, thinking hard. She remembered how, on that first day back, Toby had tried to take the suitcase from her. And then there were all those flustered, anxious looks. And the way he was always trying to get her attention, saying he had something important to tell her.

Toby!

Had he known the painting was in her suitcase? Was that why he'd offered to take it? And then, when she hadn't let him, had *he* sneaked into her room and rooted around in it when she wasn't there?

But how had poor pathetic Toby got mixed up in it all? Had the Snakes got to him somehow? Was *that* why rock-hard quiff and bushy moustache were always hanging around?

He didn't have the brains to be *in charge* of anything. He wasn't clever enough to know about old masters or tryptichs or anything like that. But he was the sort of person who could be bossed about. The kind of person who could be made to do things for other people. Unpleasant things.

A stooge. That was what they were called.

But did stooges do terrible things like cutting off people's fingers?

She couldn't imagine Toby doing something like that.

She tried to remember what the voice had sounded like on the phone that day in Hampstead. It had been muffled and yet... the person had sounded like he was talking through his nose. Adenoidal, Ronnie called it.

Just like Toby spoke. Always had.

She'd come home to Waterloo thinking she'd be safe.

But she wasn't safe.

Quick, quick. Shove her things into her case, slam it shut, buckle it up. She'd get His Nibs, go back to Hampstead despite Gam's threats. Telephone Ronnie when she got there.

Heart thudding, she half-scrambled, half-skidded down the stairs.

There he was behind the counter.

'Hurry up and change that keg, Toby!' shouted one of the customers. 'I'm thirsty!'

Caro watched as he nodded and moved towards the cellar door.

This was her chance. While he was changing the beer barrel, she could make her escape. Perhaps, before she went to Hampstead she should go to Mayfair. Lord Dockitt had said she should if she was in danger. Or even straight to the police.

She was halfway across the saloon when something stopped her.

Was she really frightened of *Toby*? She'd never been frightened of him in her life before! And then anger bloomed, replacing the fear. Ronnie had trusted him. And he had betrayed her trust.

Her eyes swept round the pub. No sign of rock-hard quiff or moustache.

In a trice, she was behind the bar and slipping through the cellar door. Carefully, she shut it behind her and there he was, at the bottom of the steps, concentrating on heaving a new beer barrel into place.

The step that she was standing on creaked and he looked up, his eyes meeting hers. He looked even more scared than she felt.

'What're you doing?' she hissed, descending the stairs.

'I'm just changing the barrel,' he said nervously.

'Not that! Following me to Hampstead... breaking into the house... phoning me...'

'Shut up!' Toby glanced fearfully beyond her, towards the top of the steps and the closed cellar door.

'Who *are* they, Toby? What're they doing here? Those leather jackets?'

'Stop it! Stop asking questions!' he said.

'Why? You going to cut my fingers off if I don't?' She wouldn't allow herself to be afraid. She couldn't.

'You need to stay out of it,' he said. His voice sounded strained, like a violin string that has been wound too tight.

'I can't,' said Caro and her voice was shaking, she was so angry. 'They've been in our pub, haven't they? The Snakes. Are you one, too?'

'No!' burst out Toby violently, forgetting to be quiet himself. 'You're wrong.'

'You're lying!' said Caro. 'Your stinky cologne gave you away. I saw it in the bathroom. Tell me why you want the painting? Is it for them?'

'You've got it, then?' said Toby, and for a minute a kind of twisted relief flooded his features. 'Give it to me, give it to me now!'

He leapt forward, clutching hold of Caro's arm.

'Let go!' With one giant shove she wrenched away from him, so suddenly that Toby staggered backwards, losing his balance and sprawling against the crates and the beer barrels.

In a flash, the fight seemed to go out of him. He put his hand to his eyes and she heard a muffled sob.

'You've got to tell me. Where is the painting, Caro?' he asked feebly.

'Safe,' said Caro, thinking of its hiding place in the car in the Rubbles.

Toby reared up again. Lurched towards her. 'Are you stupid? If you don't hand it over now, I'll . . .'

'What?' said Caro, backing away. Out of the corner of her eye she spied Jacinta's hammer hanging on the wall by the bottom of the cellar steps. Before Toby could tell what she was doing, she reached out, grasped its wooden handle, felt its weight, and held it out in front of her.

Surprise leapt into Toby's eyes.

'I'm not going to hurt you!' he said. 'I'm not like them!'

'Aren't you?'

'No!'

'Then tell me one thing,' she said, still holding the hammer out in front of her just in case. 'How did the painting get into mum's old suitcase?'

There was a short silence. Then, 'They made me put it in there.'

'They *made* you?'

'They told me to hide it somewhere incriminating. That's how the Snakes operate. Try to involve other people, innocent people. To cover themselves. Then if anything goes wrong, the blame falls on someone else.'

'Like my mum,' said Caro.

'Yeah,' said Toby.

'... So ... Mum *didn't* have anything to do with it?'

'Is that what you think?' He laughed, but it wasn't a happy laugh.

'I didn't know what to think! And you did what they asked ...' she said. She despised him!

'Thought they were my friends,' said Toby gloomily.

'Offering me all this stuff, being nice to me ... Then when they found out Mrs Rudd was away and your mum was missing, they started to use this place like their headquarters and I began to have second thoughts. 'Course I did. And then they got nasty. Really nasty. Said they'd cut off my ear – my *ear*, Caro! – and send it to my gran if I didn't do what they asked. Imagine! My gran would drop down dead with the fright of it!'

Toby shuddered and tugged at his ear, a smallish ear really, which was a bit red.

'They're thieves,' he said fiercely. 'Bad 'uns through and through. I didn't have any choice Caro. Thought that paintin' would be safe as houses. How was I to know you were gonna take the case!' He looked anguished.

'Oh, Toby!' wailed Caro.

'That's why I came to Hampstead. I didn't mean to scare you and your Great Aunt Wotsit. And when that didn't work, I tried the telephone call ...'

'And the Snakes ... they don't know yet?' asked Caro incredulously. 'That you've "lost" it?'

'If they did, I'd be dead already,' said Toby. 'They want it kept here until they've got all three of 'em.'

'All three paintings?'

'Yep. The plan is to sell 'em on the black market as

a job lot. I heard 'em say they'll make a fortune when they find the right buyer.'

'And the other two ... are the Dockitt's *Skylark* ...'

'They've got that one.'

Caro lowered the hammer, felt it swing heavily by her side.

'Where?'

'I dunno, do I? Rob or Ray's got it.'

'Rob or Ray?'

'Fellas with the perfect quiff and the moustache. You must have seen them.'

'But the third painting is in the National Gallery isn't it?'

'Not for long,' said Toby.

Caro stared at him. The whole thing was monstrous.

'So don't you see?' Toby said. 'You've *got* to tell me where *The Thrush* is. I'm begging of you. You can see the trouble I'm in!'

Chapter Seventeen

In the gloom of the cellar, Caro and Toby stared at one another. The air between them felt thick with secrets. Above them, they could hear the hubbub of conversation, the clink of glasses. Life going on as normal.

But to Caro, normality seemed a world away.

'The painting that belongs to the Dockitts, the one that Rob or Ray hid,' she said. 'You honestly don't know where it is?'

'No,' said Toby. 'And I don't want to know either. I'm already in way too deep. I wish I'd never got mixed up in it all in the first place!'

'Well, it's a bit late for that. We'll have to go to the police,' said Caro. She hung the hammer back on its hook and began to walk back up the stairs.

'You can't!' said Toby. 'Have you forgotten what I said about my ear?!'

Caro stopped. He was right. If the Snakes discovered she and Toby had told on them, they would probably cut off her finger as well as Toby's ear. She looked down at her hands. At her thin fingers, with their quite dirty fingernails, covered in cuts and grazes from her gymnastics and climbing. What if they sent one in the post to Ronnie? Or left one on a plate for Jacinta to find when she got home? Plus, if her fingers were chopped off she'd never be able to balance. *That* would put an end to her acrobatic career.

'Caro, I *hid* the thing! I practically *invited* the Snakes into Mrs Rudd's pub. I knew what was going on!' Toby's face twisted in remorse. 'Also,' he continued, speaking quickly now that he had her attention again, 'what if the police think Mrs Rudd is involved too? Bit convenient, isn't it, her being away?'

'But she's not involved!' cried Caro. She thought about Ronnie and all the stress she was under. The thought of her coming back and being accused of this! That would be horrible!

'Then give me the painting,' said Toby urgently. 'Please.'

Caro hesitated. If she went to the Rubbles and fetched the painting, then all this horror would go away.

But then she remembered that awful night in Hampstead. Even if the ghostly figure in the mirror *had* only been Toby, it had still been terrifying. And all those reports on the radio of the thefts and the threats the Snakes were involved in. If she gave in that easily, then they'd just keep on. They'd keep stealing and breaking into places and terrorising people just like they'd terrorised her and Gam.

And besides, what had Victor said? If you have a problem, face up to it. Don't think you can deal with it by running away.

An idea sparked. Just a flicker of an idea. But it was a start.

'I'll get the painting for you,' she said. Her voice sounded steady and confident, far more confident than she felt. If she could give him a painting that *looked* like the real thing, she could buy some time. And then, while the Snakes were looking the other way, she could take the genuine article to the police.

She watched as Toby's shoulders slumped in relief.

'Thanks, Caro,' he said. And he smiled at her, a genuine smile, as if she really was going to make everything all right.

* * *

It was gone four o'clock when Caro emerged from the tube. Great plops of rain had begun to fall. Within minutes it was pouring; the streets slick, the just-lit lamps making bright splashes on the shiny pavements.

His Nibs hated the rain and Caro was pleased that she had left him safely tucked up in his hutch. Instead, she had whizzed to the Rubbles, fished the painting out of its hiding place and gone straight to Horace's. In a rush she'd told him everything and asked him to keep an eye on the rabbit and any comings and goings at the pub until she returned. He had agreed.

It felt odd being back in Hampstead. She was nervous that she might bump into Gam. What would she say if she did see her? She still didn't trust her because of what had happened with His Nibs. But she knew it was more complicated than that, now that she knew about Billy and Mr Monday.

At the entrance to Heath View, Caro paused. Her

eyes swept over the brickwork all smothered in ivy, the sweep of the drive, the posts either side of the gate. And as she took it all in, for a fleeting moment she registered something new. Something different. But the rain was coming down in sheets, and her feet inside her plimsolls were starting to squelch, so she put the thought to one side, dashed across the drive, and began to swing her way up the side of the house. The window to the nursery was dark, so she continued past it, up the drainpipe to the higher window under the eaves that looked into Marks's room.

There they were. It was like a scene from a Christmas card: Tom, Marks and Albie, huddled around the gas fire, crumpets speared on the ends of toasting forks. Albie looked happy, safe. He had been right to come back with Tom, she could see that.

Caro tapped on the window, once, twice. Marks turned, her eyes widening, and then in three big strides she was across the floor, pushing up the sash and pulling Caro in, raindrops flying everywhere.

'Are you trying to give me a heart attack?' she shrieked, grabbing a towel and rubbing at Caro as if she were a wet dog. 'Why can't you use the front door like every other sane human being?'

'What is it, Caro?' asked Tom. 'Didn't expect

to see you so soon! Thought you weren't keen on coming back?'

Caro pulled the painting out from her inner cape pocket. Thank goodness it hadn't got wet.

'I need a favour,' she said to Marks. To Albie, she tried to signal a message with her eyes. *Tell you about it later.*

'Can you copy this?' She pushed the painting into Marks's hands.

'What?!' Marks held the painting at arms' length. Narrowed her eyes. Squinted at it in the manner of a professional artist. She handed it back to Caro.

'No,' she said. 'It's not my style ... plus I don't paint in oils. Where d'you get it from? And why d'you want me to copy it?'

'You taught me to paint like an old master,' piped up Albie, and Caro flashed him a grateful look. 'So you must know something about how to do it.'

'Is this the painting you were going on about before?' asked Tom.

There was a pause while the children looked at each other, wondering how much they should tell.

'It's a long story,' said Caro eventually. 'But I wouldn't ask if it wasn't really, really important. And it needs to be done quick.'

'That sounds pretty serious,' said Tom.

'How important?' asked Marks, blowing at her fringe.

'I just need it,' said Caro. 'I promise I'll explain as soon as I can.'

'Sounds like it's a matter of life and death,' said Tom. But he wasn't really concentrating on the words, thought Caro. Instead, he was smiling at Marks and she was smiling back at him.

'Please!' pleaded Caro. 'I promise I'll not ask you to do anything ever, ever again!'

'That's some promise,' said Marks, laughing. 'Anyway, the answer is still no. I've got to start making Mary's supper in a minute.'

'What're you making?' asked Albie.

'Oh, I don't know, I haven't thought yet ...'

'We'll make it,' said Caro.

'Bribery!' said Tom. His eyes were twinkling.

Caro noticed that Marks and Tom were looking at each other as though they were about to drown in each other's eyes.

'I don't have oils ...' mused Marks. 'But I suppose I could mix some egg white into the paint to give it the right effect ...'

'Egg!' said Albie, 'won't that stink?'

'Not immediately,' said Marks.

She moved over to her stack of prepared canvases. Selected one that was the correct size.

'Go on, then, why not?' she said. 'I fancy a day off cooking. You make Mary's supper and I'll do this. Tom can keep me company. Deal?'

'Deal!' said Caro. She didn't quite know how she'd swung that, but she suspected it might have something to do with ... love. Certainly Marks and Tom didn't seem quite in their right minds.

In the kitchen, Albie listened in stunned silence as Caro related all the latest happenings.

'But what'll we do next?' he asked.

'Give the fake painting to Toby and then take the real one to the police,' said Caro. It sounded so easy. So matter-of-fact. 'The Snakes won't know anything is wrong until it's too late ...'

But Albie had stopped listening. Instead he was staring out of the window, as if he'd seen a ghost.

'Stop talking!' said Albie, shushing her. 'What's that?'

Caro listened. Outside, on top of the beating rain, came the distinct sound of crunching gravel. Very carefully, Albie put the carton of eggs he had just fetched from the larder down onto the table. Slowly he turned a petrified gaze towards Caro. What if it was the Snakes? What if they'd already squeezed the truth out of Toby? What if they had followed Caro across town and were going to take the painting by force?

Caro crept towards the window and peered out. Tap, shuffle, tap shuffle. It wasn't Rob, or Ray.

'It's Gam!' she whispered. Black dress, green silk umbrella, barely discernible from the shrubs and the bushes in the fading light.

'What's *she* doing outside?' whispered Albie.

'I thought you said she had a bad back,' whispered Caro in return. There was no time to hide. Gam was already outside the door. And now the door opened, and she stepped inside. She was drenched, a puddle of rainwater collecting on the kitchen floor.

'Oh!' she said, looking up and catching sight of Caro. 'You're back.' She rubbed her wet hands on her skirt, leaving white marks on the black fabric.

'Well, not properly,' started Caro awkwardly. 'I can't...'

Caro had been about to say, 'I can't come back because you went crazy and called the RSPCA about my rabbit.' But then she saw that Gam already looked sort of crestfallen, and all of a sudden she knew she couldn't add to that sadness.

'Did you come to see Albie, then? That was kind,' Gam was saying now. Caro nodded *yes*.

Gam began to climb the stairs. She seemed to be

leaning rather heavily on her umbrella. Halfway up she stopped and turned. 'I'm sorry if I frightened you the other day.' She was speaking so quietly Caro had to take a step towards her to hear. 'It's just ... some things never stop causing pain.' Caro waited, not knowing what to say. Gam seemed to be searching for words that wouldn't come. 'Anyway, I mustn't keep you. Don't leave it too late getting back to Waterloo.'

'Great Aunt Mary ...' For a minute Caro was tempted to tell Gam everything.

'Yes, Caro?' Gam stopped. It was the first time she'd called her Caro, not Caroline, and Caro saw the same kindness on her face she'd glimpsed once before, after the break-in.

Caro opened her mouth and closed it again. It wasn't just about the rabbit. It was the great yawning chasm that stretched between her and her mother and Gam, and the something huge that had happened that had driven them apart. Something far more significant than threatening to send His Nibs to the RSPCA. It was too big. And Caro didn't know where to start.

'Nothing, doesn't matter,' she said. And did she imagine it, or did Gam's face fall?

'What time is supper, Albie?' Gam asked as she started up the stairs again.

'In a minute,' he said. 'Do you want it here or in your bedroom?'

'Drawing room, please. By the window.'

'What's *wrong* with her?' asked Caro after Gam had tapped her way up the stairs and disappeared. It was as if the rod of steel that had stretched from the toes of her leather boots all the way up to her black lace cap had vanished into thin air.

'Marks says she's been funny since you ran away,' said Albie. 'Sits and stares out of the window for hours and hours on end!'

'Does she?' said Caro. She felt confused. If what Albie was saying was true and Gam had been waiting for her, then why hadn't she begged her to stay?

'She said sorry, Caro,' said Albie.

'Yes, but...'

It still didn't make sense.

* * *

The studio end of Marks's room was awash with uncapped tubes of paint, brushes, palettes and rags. But amongst all the chaos, on her easel two identical paintings sat side by side.

'I think I've found myself a new career!' she said as Caro and Albie came in.

'She's a genius, isn't she?' said Tom admiringly.

'Oh!' said Caro. The painting was perfect. The dark-pink blossom, the speckly bird, the pale-blue sky. Surely, the Snakes would never be able to tell that this wasn't the real one?

'Thank you, Marks,' she said. 'Tom is right, you *are* a genius.'

* * *

As soon as the painting was dry, Caro set off. She was just approaching the end of Flask Walk when she saw Victor sitting on their bench.

He was all bundled up in his coats, throwing scraps of bread to the pigeons.

'Victor!' Caro's heart lifted. She rushed over and sat down next to him. 'I'm sorry I haven't been able to say thank you,' she said, 'for finishing the balancing beam and everything. It's amazing...'

'But I haven't seen you up there for days,' said Victor, puzzled. 'I wasn't sure if I'd overstepped the mark.'

'Oh, no,' said Caro hurriedly. 'You could never do that! It's just there's been a lot going on. I had to take

His Nibs away because Gam can't stand rabbits, you see. She wanted us to get rid of him!'

'Gam?' echoed Victor.

'Great Aunt Mary,' explained Caro. 'The relative who was looking after me. Not any more, though. I'm back at home now.'

Something in the air seemed to change. Victor's eyes sharpened. He looked closely at Caro. 'And where is "home"?'

'Waterloo,' she said. He seemed to be listening ever so carefully. 'The Railway Tavern, except everyone calls it Mrs Rudd's Pub.'

'But ... surely this ... Gam ... will miss you? And what about Albie?'

'She won't miss me,' said Caro firmly. 'She doesn't care about me.' Although after what had just happened in the kitchen, Caro wasn't entirely sure if that statement was true. 'Just like she didn't care about my mum,' she added.

Victor seemed to have stopped listening. He had a faraway look in his eyes. Caro jumped off the bench. The clock was ticking. Toby was waiting.

'I'll be back,' she said, 'to visit Albie, and you, and practise on the beam ... Promise!'

And she was off, running up the street and round

the corner to the tube, busy thinking about how long it would take to get back to Waterloo, and what she would say to Toby, and if he and the Snakes would be taken in by the fake painting and not find out about the real one, nestling alongside it in her pocket.

* * *

It wasn't until Caro was on the southbound train that she remembered the thing she had seen outside the house. The 'something' that was new.

It had been on the gatepost. A chalk mark. An upside-down V with a line across the top.

The rain had been pelting down and it was half dark. But she *had* seen it.

The welcome sign. The sign that Victor had said meant a household was exceptionally friendly – providing a hot meal and sometimes even shelter – to the gentlemen of the road.

Had Albie put it there? He most probably had, given how much he'd loved Victor's stories, especially the ones about the tramps' travelling code. She should have told Victor. Albie would have been thrilled to have given him some supplies.

Mind you, Gam wouldn't be too happy. It was bound

to be one of the many things she disapproved of. In fact, it might even have shocked her into being more like her cantankerous old self.

Chapter Eighteen

When she got back to Waterloo, Caro went straight to the Rubbles to hide the real painting in the derelict car. Then she made her way to the pub.

As soon as she slipped through the doors into the saloon bar, she knew something was wrong.

It was the quietness that alarmed her. A sort of ominous quiet. Like the stillness you get before a storm.

Usually at this time, Ronnie and Toby would be buzzing about, wiping down the tables, washing the glasses, totting up the evening's takings at the till.

But tonight there was no one to be seen and the

place was a mess: dirty glasses littering the tables, overflowing ash trays cluttering the bar.

Swiftly Caro picked her way across the room. She could hear voices coming from the kitchen, and... her skin prickled. Was that a moan?

Streaks of light glimmered between the strands of beaded curtain that separated the kitchen from the bar. Caro crept closer; the moan came again, a pitiful sound, like an animal in pain, and then a rough voice saying, 'Hurts, don't it?'

'Yes...' The reply was half-gasped, half-whispered. Toby.

'Where is it, boy?'

A female voice. Brittle and sharp, like shards of broken glass.

'I told you to keep it safe and you couldn't even do that. *What've* you done with it?'

Very carefully, Caro parted the beaded curtain just enough so that she could see, but not be seen.

A glimpse of an elegant wrist clutching at Toby's throat.

An elegant wrist with a tattoo of a snake curling round it.

Caro pressed a fist to her mouth to stifle a scream. Her eyes grew wide. Emerald! Toby's own *mother*? Was *she* a Snake?

The Queen of the Snakes?

Living in Mrs Rudd's Pub? Sleeping in Ronnie and Jacinta's bed?

Trusted to look after the place ...

Don't cry, Caro, don't cry. Stay calm. Don't let her see you.

Why hadn't Toby told her the whole truth?

She could see them through the beaded strands. A grotesque tableau: Emerald and the two leather-jacketed men hunched around Toby, who was leaning against the sink, his arm twisted at an odd angle behind his back.

So Toby hadn't told her everything. But equally, she hadn't asked. She'd just assumed when he spoke about the Snakes, he was talking about Rob and Ray.

A wave of sheer panic reared up into her chest, to her throat.

She was so scared she thought she was going to be sick.

'I *said*,' said Emerald, making a grab for Ronnie's best cut-glass vase, the one Jacinta had given her for her birthday, '*what* have you done with it?'

'I can't ...'

The vase went hurtling through the air, smashing into the wall opposite and shattering into a million pieces on the kitchen floor.

Caro instinctively took a step back. The hand that was parting the curtains started to shake.

'Spit it out,' growled Rob. 'Or were you born useless?' He jerked at Toby's arm again, higher and harder, and this time Toby cried out in pain.

'Where. Have. You. Put. The. Painting?' Emerald spat out each word like it was a poisoned dart.

They must've come looking for the painting while Caro was out. Maybe if she hadn't stopped to talk to Victor she could have been back in time...

'I don't know,' stuttered Toby and Caro winced. She could see there were bruises on his neck. His head was down. His gaze fixed on the floor. He looked like he wanted to disappear.

And even though he had been stupid; even though he had betrayed Ronnie's trust... Caro felt a flicker of sympathy. She could see he was petrified. She could almost smell his fear.

But if she went in there now, what would happen to *her*?

If she showed them the fake painting and they guessed it was a trick... Would she ever come back out?

'Need a little more persuading, do you?' hissed Emerald.

Something sparked in Ray's hand. A flash of silver. The gleam of a flick knife.

'Stop!' shouted Caro, the word out of her mouth even before she'd had time to think it. And now she crashed through the beads, unable to watch any longer.

Emerald whipped round.

'What,' she said, 'are you doing here? I thought we had an agreement. You stay out of my way and I'll stay out of yours.'

Caro flinched. The woman in front of her was the same... but different. She stared at Caro threateningly.

'I know, but—'

'Can't you see we're in the middle of some business,' interrupted Emerald. 'And it's nothing that concerns you!' There was something about her. Something very dangerous that was only seconds away from boiling over.

'But it *does* concern me,' said Caro quickly. Too late to change her mind now.

'You're not making this easy are you?' sighed Emerald. 'Get rid of her, Rob.'

'No!' said Caro.

But Rob had already crossed the kitchen and taken a rough hold of Caro's arm.

'But it's not Toby's fault,' burst out Caro.

'I *told* you to keep out of the way—'

'The painting you're talking about,' gabbled Caro.

They were all staring at her. Three pairs of cruel, mean eyes. And Toby's terrified ones.

Something ignited in Emerald and, in a flash, she grabbed hold of Toby and dragged him towards her so that his face was inches from hers.

'Have you been blabbing?' she screamed. 'Do you *want* to end up at the bottom of the Thames?'

'Don't!' shouted Caro. She was properly frightened now. Emerald's eyes were glittering so strangely. What was she capable of?

Caro didn't want to find out.

'I took it,' she said. There, the words were out.

'You *what*?'

Emerald released Toby. Turned to Caro. Her gaze so full of menace it sent shivers up Caro's spine.

'I took it by mistake,' said Caro quickly. 'I didn't know it was in that suitcase. And I didn't find it until I got to Hampstead. How was I to know it was yours?'

'She's telling the truth,' cut in Toby nervously. 'I hid it there, safe, in an "*incriminating*" place just like you told me to, but when I went to get it, it wasn't there any more...'

Emerald boxed Toby's ears hard.

'Why didn't you say that in the first place, you idiot? Protecting her, were you? You're pathetic.'

'I didn't mean to—' mumbled Toby.

'Because *I* told him it would be all right,' interrupted Caro. 'He was scared of what you'd do – and anyway, the painting is quite safe.'

'If it's so safe, where is it?'

Emerald nodded at Rob and Ray, and they moved so that they were blocking both exits – the door to the yard and the door leading back into the pub.

'Here,' said Caro. She stuck her hand inside her cape, feeling for the inner pocket and withdrew the painting.

Emerald's hand shot out and snatched it.

'Will you leave us alone now?' Caro asked. Every cell in her body was screaming at her to run, run as fast as she could, away from this place, away from this danger. But she stayed where she was. She had to see this through.

Emerald didn't reply. Instead, she slowly unwrapped the painting. Held it at arm's length. Then brought it close, her eyes flickering over it greedily. Caro felt like she could barely breathe.

'Not a word,' said Emerald softly, her eyes flicking from Caro to Toby, 'are you to utter to anyone about this. Understood?'

The blade was still gleaming in Ray's hand.

Toby nodded his head frantically. 'Not a word, honest, not a word...'

'If I suspect you of *anything* – anything at all – I can bring this pub down. Are you listening?' She was looking at Caro now.

Caro jerked her head, yes. She believed every word Emerald was saying.

'Your mother will come back to nothing, understand? No more cosy life here with you and the other one – Veronica doo dah. You'll be out on the streets.'

Her gaze was cold, her words like a winter blizzard.

'You'd best remember,' she continued, 'I have contacts *everywhere*. I could put a halt to madam's whistling career just like that' – she clicked her fingers – 'if I wanted to...'

'Well, you won't need to,' said Caro. 'Toby just said we won't tell – and we won't.'

'Good.' There was a pause, and then she fluttered her fingers in the direction of the stairs. 'Now, to bed. We'll decide what to do with you in the morning.'

'But His Nibs...' Caro couldn't help saying. She should check that he was all right. Give him some fresh hay.

'Bugs Bunny,' said Emerald grimly, 'is perfectly all right. Rob, escort them upstairs. And make sure they go straight to their rooms. There'll be no conspiring tonight.'

* * *

All through the night Caro tossed and turned. She slept in fits and starts, her mind buzzing – vibrating almost – alive with thoughts and feelings, prodding and stabbing, and whizzing round and round her head like flying knives. She detested Emerald – detested her with a venom that she had never felt before. For threatening to close the pub and destroy Jacinta Monday's whistling career; for hurting Toby; for frightening the living daylights out of *her*.

Any minute now she might re-examine the painting. Work out it was a fake. And then what would happen? Would *Caro* end up in the Thames? She hadn't forgotten that threat, or the silver blade. How long did she have before Emerald twigged that something was wrong?

It had been impossible to catch Toby's eye as Rob had herded them up to their bedrooms. And when Caro had tried to sneak out of her room later, she'd been shocked to find Ray standing sentry outside. He had growled at her, showing a full set of black teeth, and she had retreated fast.

Then she'd rushed straight over to her window, ready to make her escape that way instead. But a telltale coil of smoke had drifted up in the black night air and she had backed off. Either Emerald was down there, or Rob. Either way, she couldn't risk climbing down just yet.

Back in bed, Caro lay with her eyes wide open, staring into the dark. The plan had been to give the painting to Toby and then go straight to the police with the other one. But how could she do that now?

When the first sludgy signs of morning crept in through her window, Caro slipped out of bed. In the room next door, the bed creaked. Emerald. Just the thought of her made Caro's blood run cold. Avoiding the creaky floorboards, she tiptoed to the door. But now when she tried the door handle, it was locked. And if she was locked in, Toby probably was, too.

The floorboards were chilly on her bare feet as she crept over to the window. Outside, everything was cloaked in a thick, yellowy-grey fog. She couldn't see *anything*, not the yard, nor the hutch or the back gate. Quickly, she grabbed her jeans and her sweater and pulled them on. She pushed the window up. It squeaked a complaint, but thankfully the squeak was drowned out by a train rumbling slowly past.

Out on the window ledge, the mist swirled and curled. Caro stretched up, fingers blindly searching for the gutter. It was what she grabbed hold of to swing herself up and onto the roof. But where was it? A loose slate clattered down to the yard below and Caro froze, waiting for Emerald's window to screech open, and her razor-sharp voice to split the air. But ... nothing. The porridge-like fog was good at deadening sound, and all around remained silent and still.

There! Her fingers found the hold they were looking for, and she hoisted herself up, scrambling onto the slippery, moss-covered tiles. Through the gloom she could just see a faint light in Toby's attic window. If she stretched out and inched her way up diagonally, she could do it.

Slowly, she half crawled, half shunted her body up the slope of the roof until she was level with the tiny window. She scratched at the glass. Nothing. She knocked, but the sound was muffled by the fog. Gripping the narrow window ledge with one hand, she felt in her pocket with the other. Found a coin. Tapped it on the glass. Chink, chink, chink.

The light brightened, and a ghostly face appeared on the other side of the glass.

Very carefully, Toby prised the window open so

that he didn't knock Caro backwards. His eyes darted about, as though at any moment the leather jackets or Emerald might appear.

She could still see the marks on his neck. The bruises that had turned a dark shade of purple. A red weal decorated his cheek

'You lied to me,' she said. 'And to Ronnie. About Emerald Standing being your mother. You could've told me yesterday!'

'I was scared,' he said. 'I've been *so* scared Caro...'

'Well, I'm scared too!' she said. 'How could you? Ronnie trusted you!'

'No one ever liked me. You and Mrs Rudd despised me...'

'We didn't!' Or had they? They'd never had much time for him, that was for sure.

'And then Rob and Ray came along and they treated me with respect. And Mrs Standing, she promised me all kinds of stuff... she said if I worked for her I'd have more luck with girls...'

Even though Caro was scared, that made her laugh.

'You did all this to get a girlfriend?!'

'It's all right for you to laugh,' said Toby, looking injured. 'You've got two mums, *and* Horace, and your gymnastics.'

'Oh, Toby,' said Caro. She wanted to say, 'Stop feeling sorry for yourself,' but she could already see he had tortured himself enough with what he had done.

'The worst thing is,' said Toby, 'she's talkin' about pinning the whole thing on Mrs Rudd. Says she can spin it so as the cops think your Ronnie was using her sick sister as a cover. The Snakes can frame people – easy. They've done it before and they'll do it again. Once the National Gallery raid is done, the pub will be a goner.'

'She can't do that!' Caro burned with the injustice of it. Whichever way you looked at it, it seemed like everyone and everything was doomed. 'I'm going to the police station right now, Toby, I have to.'

'But ...' and she knew he was going to say something about sheared-off fingers and lopped-off ears and bodies being thrown into the Thames, but she wouldn't listen, she couldn't listen. She mustn't let the threats frighten her.

'I'm going,' she cut him off. 'But first ... promise me something?'

'Yes?'

'If I don't come back, or the police don't turn up, you *must* get out of here somehow. Phone Ronnie, tell her what's been going on, and get her to come home. Promise?'

'Promise,' said Toby earnestly. 'I won't let you down this time.'

* * *

By the time Caro had climbed down to the yard, the fog was thinning. She could see the hutch now. She would take His Nibs with her to the police station. When he was in her arms, she didn't feel so scared.

Her hands were deep in the hay, feeling for the warmth of her rabbit when behind her the kitchen door swung open.

Caro became very still. She heard the distinct sound of a disappointed sigh. She didn't dare turn round.

'Tell me, are you looking for something?'

Chapter Nineteen

It was Emerald, staring at her as though she would gladly chop off every single one of Caro's fingers right now.

'Looking for Bugs Bunny?'

'He's not called that,' said Caro fiercely. She hated this woman who had scared Toby into doing something really stupid. Who was planning to wreck Ronnie's life with her false accusations. Who thought it was completely OK to shatter beautiful vases and use knives to threaten people.

'Pardon *me*,' said Emerald. 'So . . . *are* you looking for His Highness or whatever it is you call him?'

'Yes,' said Caro. Her teeth were chattering.

She clamped her jaw tight shut. She must not be intimidated. 'And for your information, his name is His Nibs.'

Emerald Standing's eyes were like hard little pebbles.

'Well, don't let me stop you. Do carry on.'

For a second, Caro felt confused; Emerald's gaze was so strange and ... She turned back to the hutch, reached in, and all of a sudden she just knew: knew that Emerald Standing had done something worse than terrible, something unforgivable, and she plunged her hands deep into the hay and there was nothing, nothing, no warm fur, no twitching nose, no floppy ears or snuffled greeting.

The hutch was empty.

'Where is he?' She was trembling. Her chest felt like it was ... cracking.

'Wouldn't you like to know?' said Emerald.

'But why?' Caro's voice rose. 'I *promised* I wouldn't say anything!'

'Promises, promises,' said Emerald bluntly. 'How can I trust someone who sneaks out of their room via *the window*, scuttles all over the place like a spider, tries to plot God knows what with that sad excuse of a lad ...?'

Caro felt like she was about to explode.

'What have you done to him? Where is he?' she

screamed and she flew at Emerald in a blind fury, fists pounding, fingernails scratching. But it was no good. Emerald held her off, her arms as strong as iron, her face grim.

'Safe,' she said and she actually smiled as she said it.

'Safe where?'

'You'll have to trust me on that one.'

'I shall *never* trust you,' spat Caro. 'I saw your tattoo and I know who you are! And I'm going to the police right now.'

She turned to go, but as she did, Emerald grabbed her by the wrist and jerked her back.

'Do that and Bugs Bunny will be ...' She mimed slitting her throat.

'You wouldn't!' But Caro knew she would. Anyone who chopped off fingers and ears and sent them in the post could kill a rabbit, no problem.

'Help me out and you'll get your precious bunny back this evening.'

'Help you?' said Caro. Had she heard that right?

'I said when I first met you that I'd heard you were rather good at climbing.'

'What's it got to do with you?' asked Caro. She didn't like the horrible expression on Emerald's face. Sly and mean and calculating.

'I could do with a climber. For our next job. Just a small matter of breaking and entering.'

Caro recoiled.

'You're mad!'

Emerald laughed. A brittle sound. 'Some people say so.'

'I won't do it! What makes you think I would?'

'Don't want Flopsy then?'

'Of course I do! Where have you put him?'

'As I said. You do a little something for me, and I'll do a little something for you.'

Caro stared. Emerald stared back, her eyes dark, black coal pits.

'No!' Caro shouted, and then she was jerking out of Emerald's grasp, running, out of the yard through the kitchen, across the deserted saloon – still a mess – and out onto the street.

She had to find His Nibs *now*. She couldn't wait until tonight! She had told Gam she'd *die* if he was abandoned on Hampstead Heath. She felt like she was dying now.

She ran and ran and ran. To the hole in the wall, into the Rubbles.

'Look at the baby crying!'

It was the Bully Boys. Smirking and smiling. Lurking by the tyre swings.

'Shut up!' she yelled.

'All right, keep yer hair on,' said Frank, the biggest one.

Caro screamed. The longest, loudest scream in the world. A scream that contained all the secrets that Emerald wanted her to keep bottled up.

Until she found her rabbit.

The Bully Boys looked shocked. For once stunned into silence.

''Ere, you OK?' asked Stanley, the middle one, after Caro had finally stopped screaming.

'She ain't right in the head,' said Frank.

Caro lunged at him, grabbing him by the lapels.

''Ere gerroff! What you doin'?'

'Have you seen my rabbit?' she shrieked.

And then she remembered yesterday, how she and Horace had watched the leather jackets talking to the Bully Boys; the way they'd seemed to be threatening them. Had they been giving them instructions? Instructions to get rid of His Nibs?

'Nah!' said Frank, wrenching away from her.

'I ain't neither,' said Stanley.

It was the most they had ever said to one another in their entire lives.

'Have *you*?' urged Caro, appealing to the smallest

one, Carl, fighting to swallow down her sobs. It was pointless. They were enemies. Why would they help her?

But before the smallest one could formulate an answer, he was interrupted by the sound of running footsteps, and through the hole in the wall came Horace.

'Caro, was that you screaming? What did they do to you?' He was looking at the Bully Boys in disgust.

'It's Emerald. She's done something to His Nibs!' Caro cried, and the panic was back, full force, her voice high, wailing almost. She pointed a wobbly finger at the Bully Boys. 'They're working for her; I know they are. I bet they did her dirty work for her!'

In one lunge, Horace grabbed Frank and got him into a headlock.

'Give her rabbit back,' he said.

Stanley went to wrench Horace off Frank, but Caro stuck out her ankle and tripped him up.

As he fell, a scrap of paper escaped his pocket and fluttered to the ground. Caro stamped on it, trapping it with her foot just as Carl reached down to snatch it up.

'Don't,' she said. She stooped to pick it up herself. Unfolded it. Read the scrawled words.

12.00 P.M. NATIONAL GALLERY. ROOM 17A.

The National Gallery? Was that the 'little job' Emerald had just asked her to help with?

'What's this?' she asked, looking up at the Bully Boys 'You too?'

There was a silence.

She passed the note to Horace.

'Tell me!' she shouted. 'Are you in with the Snakes, too?'

'It's not like that,' muttered Frank.

Horace stepped forward with his fists up.

'You'd better talk,' he said. 'Or else.'

'It's the raid to steal the third bird painting, isn't it?' said Caro. Emerald Standing was omnipotent. She had everyone in her clutches.

'They paid us a few bob,' admitted Carl. 'To have a fight. Inside the gallery. Don't know why.'

'They said don't blab!' Frank said, kicking Carl in the shins.

'They said they'd kill us if we did!' said Stanley.

'Now you've done it!' said Frank. 'They'll close down Mum's shop ...'

His mum's shop. The tobacconist's by the station.

'And Dad's milk round,' said Stanley.

Caro stared. And all of a sudden she saw that they were frightened. Like she was frightened. Out of their depth. *All* of them at the mercy of Emerald Standing.

Horace lowered his fists. Glanced over to Caro for affirmation. He knew too. This wasn't the time for fighting.

Could they be on the same side?

'Do you *want* them to do all those things?' asked Caro. 'Close your mum's shop? Ruin your dad's milk round?'

'They won't if we do what they asked ...' Stanley stuttered.

'They will!' yelled Caro. 'And they'll go on and on, making life miserable for anyone who gets in their way – don't you *ever* listen to the news?'

'Tell us where the rabbit is,' said Horace, calm as anything.

'The Snakes got him,' said Carl.

'They was walkin' up there,' said Stanley. 'Towards the shot tower. They might have been holding something furry. Maybe.'

The shot tower! Caro turned a stricken face to Horace. What had they taken him there for? To hurl him off the top?

She could barely think for the deafening sound of blood pounding in her ears.

There was no reason to trust the Bully Boys, to expect any help from them given their past record, but it was worth a try.

'Don't say anything. Go along with the plan for now. The fight in Room 17a at twelve o'clock. All right?'

Amazingly, they nodded.

'C'mon,' she said to Horace. And they ran.

* * *

For as long as Caro had been alive, and even a hundred years before that, the shot tower had loomed large over her patch of Lambeth. It was just there, always had been, a place once busy with shot makers plying their trade, pouring molten lead from a great height all the way down to the water trough below, where it miraculously formed itself into hundreds and thousands of tiny little globes: shot for muskets and sporting guns.

Now it stood empty, disused for two decades or more, the Royal Festival Hall built right on top of its cobbled works yard. No more furnaces burning, no more cleaning and stirring, no more drying and polishing. The old men who had operated it, top and bottom, were long gone. The tower, however, remained.

Caro and her friends had often cricked their necks to see all the way to the parapet at the top. They had imagined what it would be like up there, high, high in the sky. The view would be stupendous. You'd be able to see for miles. But the door at the bottom had always been bolted, and the three-foot-thick brick wall defied climbing, the tower's narrow windows too high and too far apart to be of any use, even for an extraordinary climber like Caro.

Today the door was locked as it always was. Caro pulled it, pummelled it, kicked it, hurled her whole body at it. It wouldn't budge.

'Careful, Caro,' said Horace. He fished several pencils out of his pocket and tried to jemmy the door with them, but he didn't have a clue what he was doing and the pencils snapped in his hands.

Caro threw herself at the walls and tried to scrabble up them, but there were no footholds. Not one. It was impossible!

His Nibs was in there. Locked up. Wondering where she was. She could just picture the worried twitch of his ears, the sad blink of his eyes. Her heart seemed to fold in on itself. There was no way she could get to him.

'I'm going to have to do it, Horace,' she said, turning her back on the tower and starting to stride away. 'I'll have to "help" her as she puts it. It's the only way I'll get His Nibs back.'

'Emerald Standing?' Horace said.

'Indeed,' said Caro.

'But you can't trust her!' cried Horace, running after her. 'She won't keep her word...'

Caro knew that Horace was right. You could *never* trust a person like Emerald Standing. She would creep up on you and stab you in the back and take everything you loved before you even knew it.

But Caro wouldn't *let* her take everything. She would fight tooth and nail for His Nibs, for Ronnie, for Jacinta and the pub.

'She'd better keep her word,' said Caro. 'Or else...' Or else what?

On the other side of the Thames, Big Ben struck ten.

'I'm coming with you, then,' said Horace.

'No.' Caro stopped walking and turned to face him. If this all went wrong, and she got caught and... what? Sent to prison? Did twelve-year-old girls get sent to prison? No, she would be sent to an approved school, horrible places where children were sent if they had committed a crime. There'd be no rabbits in an approved school, and nowhere to practise gymnastics, and no Ronnie and no Mum.

And if Horace was sent there? It was too dreadful to imagine. He had already done enough for her. She couldn't risk putting him through that too.

'No, Horace,' she said. 'I've got to do this on my own.'

Chapter Twenty

'I thought you'd be back,' said Emerald as Caro entered the pub. She was sitting at one of the small tables drinking a glass of what looked like Ronnie's best sherry and reading a newspaper.

There were no customers. The doors didn't open until eleven. But somehow Caro knew they were going to stay firmly shut today.

Emerald batted the newspaper out so that Caro could clearly see the front page.

'The Snakes still elude Scotland Yard,' blasted the headline.

'I take it you're in then?' asked Emerald.

Caro hesitated. Was she about to make the biggest

mistake of her life? Maybe. But she didn't see any alternative right now.

She folded her arms and nodded. 'I'm in.'

'Good. Now listen carefully, we haven't got long. You will enter the National Gallery via the rear of the building.'

'I'll go the best way for climbing,' objected Caro. If she was going to do it, she was going to do it her way.

'You'll listen to me and do as I say,' said Emerald crisply. 'Ever taken part in a heist before?'

Caro shook her head, *no*. Of course she hadn't!

'Thought not,' said Emerald. 'So you'll do as planned. And I will not tolerate you messing it up. OK?'

'OK,' said Caro. *Just agree*, she said to herself. Play along. Then maybe...

'Orange Street, the Charing Cross Road end,' Emerald rapped out. 'Get over the back wall.'

No mention of *how* she should get over the back wall, thought Caro. She was about to ask but, seeing Emerald Standing's grim expression, decided against it.

'Then enter via the first floor. There's a small window to the right of the third drainpipe along. Clear?'

'Clear,' said Caro.

'It'll be unlocked. You'll find yourself in the ladies' lavatories. Wait there until three minutes to twelve.

It will take precisely two minutes to get from there to Room 17a.'

'But,' said Caro, unable to resist another question, 'why can't I just go in the normal way? Walk in there like everyone else?'

'You'll go in the way you're going to come out,' snapped Emerald. 'Now do concentrate. *The Nightingale* looks like this.'

Emerald held up a print of a bird painting that looked very similar to *The Thrush*, except this bird looked plainer, with brown wings and a slightly reddish tail; and instead of being surrounded by dark-pink blossom, it was sitting on a single plain twig.

Jacinta Monday could whistle a perfect imitation of the nightingale's song, and Caro had imagined that a bird that sang so beautifully might look a bit prettier. The bird in the print had a charming little beak though, which was wide open as if it was in mid-song. Or waiting for its mother to feed it.

'Are you paying attention?' barked Emerald.

'Yes,' said Caro.

'Rob and Ray will be there,' continued Mrs Standing. 'And they'll be watching you. As soon as you've got the painting, you'll exit the way you entered. Got it? One step out of line and Bugs Bunny will be history.'

She gave an especially sinister smile. 'It's a *very* long fall from the top of the shot tower you know.'

* * *

Less than thirty minutes after receiving her instructions, Caro arrived in Orange Street. It was a narrow road, mainly used for deliveries, but at this moment in time, all was quiet and not a soul was to be seen.

Carefully, Caro surveyed the joint she was about to break into. A high wall separated her from the back of the gallery. No matter. A conveniently placed parking meter would provide the perfect launch pad. From there, it would be easy to hop onto the wall and jump down to the other side.

But just as Caro was about to commence operations, a man in overalls rounded the corner. Swiftly, Caro bent down to tie her shoelace. She needn't have bothered. The man didn't so much as glance in her direction. Without the presence of His Nibs, or the dash and elegance of Horace, she blended into the background quite easily – a bit like the nightingale in the painting she was about to steal.

As soon as the man had disappeared, Caro climbed onto the parking meter, made the short leap to the top of the wall and then dropped down to the other side.

The third drainpipe along was exactly where Emerald had said it was, and conveniently, a delivery van was parked in front of it, which provided plenty of cover for Caro as she shinned up to the first floor.

From there it was a short stretch to a small, unlocked window. Caro wriggled inside and landed with a thump on the floor of the ladies' lavatories. Quick as a flash, she darted into the first cubicle and slid the bolt. Then, exercising the utmost caution, she stood on the toilet seat, so that if anyone came in, they wouldn't see her feet if they happened to crouch down and peer through the gap between the floor and the door.

She looked at her watch. Almost half an hour to go. She was so nervous it was hard to keep still, and her mind jumped ahead, unable to tear itself away from imagining all the mind-blowing 'what ifs'. What if she got caught? What if they wouldn't let her explain? What if Emerald carried out her threat to hurl His Nibs off the top of the shot tower? Or what if (fingers crossed) she forgot about him in the middle of all the rumpus?

If she did forget about it, would the authorities

take pity on Caro and let her take her rabbit to the approved school?

She stuck her hand in her pocket and pulled out the rabbit book she had taken from Tom's bedroom just two days before. Billy's book. Gam's *son's* book. She flicked through it and ... caught her breath in surprise.

How come she hadn't noticed that before?

Wherever the word 'rabbit' appeared, someone had crossed it out and in red crayon written 'Ginger' in tiny handwriting instead.

She rifled through the pages. On the back cover, in the same red crayon, were the words 'Billy and Ginger Monday.'

In the cubicle, perched on top of the toilet, Caro went very still.

Ginger!

That day when she'd met Victor for the second time, in the Wilds, for a brief moment when he'd woken up, hadn't he mistaken His Nibs for someone or something called *Ginger*?

Had he meant a *rabbit* called Ginger?

Caro's mind whirled as things started to slot into place. Billy. Ginger. Victor. *Gam*? The thought was so improbable ... and yet ...

She thought about Gam and her reaction to His Nibs. About the rusty old cage that had been in the shed.

She remembered Tom telling them that Mr Monday, Gam's husband (Billy's dad, Jacinta's uncle), could whistle anything. How he and Jacinta and Billy whistled together, all three of them. Mary, he'd said, pretended it drove her mad but she loved it really.

She recalled the day when she and Horace had run up to the Wilds to collect Jacinta's tools from the hollow in the tree trunk. And how she'd heard someone whistling and she'd thought it was her mum, but there had been no one there.

The balancing beam had been finished though.

Victor had told them that he came back to London from time to time to ... to what? He had never finished the sentence; she remembered that now.

Who or what had he come to see?

Caro's mind darted ahead. To Victor sitting on the bench at the top of Flask Walk. To Gam coming in from the rain and wiping her hands on her skirt.

Leaving white marks,

Chalk marks.

Had *Gam* put those marks on the gatepost? The tramps' 'welcome' sign?

If Victor *was* Mr Monday, then did Gam know he was a tramp?

Tom thought Mr Monday had died in the war. Well, what if he hadn't?!

Victor had told Albie how gentlemen went on the road because they couldn't face up to things. How they went walkabout to get away from difficult circumstances.

What had he said?

The words came back to Caro with perfect clarity.

'You see, that's what I did, and I regret it every day.'

Was Gam looking for Victor? Was the 'welcome' sign meant for him? Is that why she had been sitting for hours on end looking out of the window, just as Albie had said she had? Not looking for Caro, but for Victor?

Caro was so lost in thought she had forgotten about the time. Now she looked at her watch and a cold hand seemed to clutch at her throat, squeezing all the air out of her.

It was already two minutes to twelve.

* * *

In a panic, Caro raced through a series of galleries, past paintings of battles and shipwrecks and biblical scenes. Into the next gallery and the one beyond that: no leather jackets, no Bully Boys, just room after room full of gilt-framed paintings of horses and hunting dogs, ruins and temples and endless portraits of pale-faced people dressed in velvets and furs.

'Hey!' shouted a guard as Caro streaked past. 'No running allowed!'

Caro carried on. Past massive portraits of Charles I and Madame de Pompadour, and then smaller scenes of wheatfields and windmills and—

There it was, Room 17a, and it was packed with people: mums, dads, children and grandparents, all clustered around a lanky tour guide talking earnestly about a pair of paintings depicting butterflies and forget-me-nots.

Caro's gaze flashed round the room. It was so stuffed with people she could barely see the paintings on the walls, and those that she could see were tiny, not much bigger than a medium-sized adult's hand ... flowers and insects and ... It was all nature stuff but where was *The Nightingale*, and anyway, how was she meant to take it with all these people in here? She scanned the room again, searching, searching, but she couldn't see the painting and as far as she could tell, there was no sign of the leather jackets or the Bully Boys either.

From another gallery came the sound of a clock chiming twelve, and immediately there was a shout and a scuffle and – here they were! The Bully Boys bursting out from the crowd, as if they were mechanical toys and someone had wound them up, and then they were throwing actual punches and kicking each other in the shins and the tour guide issued a shocked, 'Excuse me!' and the parents gasped and gathered their children to them, shouting things like, 'Thugs! What are they doing in here?' and 'Who let them in?' and—

This was Caro's chance.

'Guards, where are the guards?' shouted the lanky tour guide.

And there they were, two of them, marshalling the crowd, herding them out of 17a and into the larger gallery beyond.

'Everyone out, please.'

The crowd shuffling out, the tour guide apologising profusely, until the only people left were the security guards, one with a shiny, rock-hard quiff, and the other with a bushy moustache. The Bully Boys stopped fighting and stood there, red-faced and panting.

Now Caro had a clear view of the paintings on the walls.

And there it was ... a plain-looking brown bird perched on a twig, nestled between paintings of a squirrel eating a nut and a vase of red tulips.

'What you waitin' for?' muttered Ray. 'Get it now and then scarper.'

A moment of stillness, of silence.

And then Caro was doing it, she was actually *doing* it, reaching up, plucking the painting from its place, popping it inside her cape and skittering into the gallery next door to join the milling crowd.

She couldn't quite believe what she had just done. It was audacious. Ludicrous. Was she actually going to get away with it?

'Caro!'

She jumped.

It was Albie, sidling up to her and speaking out of the corner of his mouth like a character in a spy movie.

'What're you doing here?' she whispered. Had anyone seen? Did she look suspicious?

Behind him she caught a glimpse of Horace running away, down the stairs.

'And what's Horace doing? I told him you two shouldn't get involved ...'

'Don't worry,' Albie whispered. 'We're here to take care of those two,' he cocked his head in the direction of the gallery where Rob and Ray were still ensconced. 'Here, take this.'

He pushed his old-fashioned rucksack into her hands.

'Why? What do I want this for?'

'Just take it Caro. You might need it.'

What was he talking about?

'Albie,' she said urgently, remembering her revelation in the ladies' lavatories. 'Can you do something for me?'

'Yes?' His eyes were alight. He seemed alive. Completely different from the shadow of that quiet, sad little boy she had first met two weeks ago.

'Fetch Victor please?'

'Victor? Why?'

'I have to ask him something. It's really important. Tell him to meet me at the pub.'

Albie nodded yes, because he trusted Caro implicitly; she was like his big sister, his *beloved* big sister, and he would do anything for her, *anything*, and then she was slipping away, away from the crowd, flitting through the galleries, back to the ladies' lavatories and her escape.

Chapter Twenty-One

Caro ran.

Across Trafalgar Square, onto the Strand, down Villiers Street, and up onto Hungerford Bridge.

The black waters of the Thames swirled vigorously; a train screeched its way into Charing Cross; Caro's heart pounded nineteen to the dozen as she clattered down the stairs on the far side of the bridge and turned towards the Royal Festival Hall.

Outside the shot tower a woman was waiting. A drab-looking woman in a headscarf and round tinted spectacles. She was clutching a pram.

Horace's pram.

'Give me the painting, quick.' A brittle voice. A harsh voice.

It was Emerald. Of course it was.

'When you've opened the door,' said Caro, still panting.

'Oh, for goodness' sake,' said Emerald. 'I haven't got time to play games. You'll get your rabbit when you've given me the painting.'

Caro hesitated. What if Emerald tricked her? Horace had said she couldn't be trusted and he was right.

But what else could she do?

Caro reached into her cape and handed the painting over.

Emerald Standing produced a key from the pocket of her raincoat.

Waved it in Caro's face.

Caro grabbed at it.

Emerald snatched it back.

'Give it to me, you traitor.' The words that shot out of Emerald Standing's mouth startled Caro, like a razor blade, scraping glass.

'What do you mean?' she said, confused. 'I just gave you the painting!'

'Do you think I'm stupid? I'm talking about *The Thrush*, you idiot. The *real* one. The one you've got.'

A pause while a cold stone dropped to the bottom of Caro's stomach.

How long had she known? The whole time?

'I *know*,' said Emerald slowly, 'that the one you gave me was a fake.'

'I haven't got it,' said Caro. It was true. She didn't. It was squashed into the hole in the red leather seat of the abandoned car in the Rubbles, the one with the exploding yellow foam.

'Dare to cross a Snake, do you?' hissed Emerald Standing.

She was too clever! Too clever by half. Always one step ahead. It wasn't fair!

Now she was holding up a hand and counting on her fingers. Her red-painted nails like beacons, flashing danger.

'Rabbit. Pub. Your two ... mothers. Want to save them? Or not?'

Caro stared at her.

'In the car, in the Rubbles,' she blurted out. 'You won't get away with this though.'

'Oh, I already have, darling.'

Caro watched helplessly as Emerald Standing tucked the painting inside the pram alongside another one. Presumably the Dockitts' *Skylark*.

Only then did she unlock the door to the shot tower.

'There you are then. Thank you, for the use of the pub and for your climbing expertise. You've been a great help.' Her voice was dripping honey now she had what she wanted.

But there was no answer from Caro. She was already running up the spiral staircase towards her rabbit, so fast that she didn't even hear Mrs Standing very deliberately slam the door shut and lock it after her.

***

There was no immediate sign of His Nibs. The spiral staircase clung to the tower walls and Caro bounded up it, round and round, counting the steps as she went. One hundred, one hundred and fifty, past a little landing known as the first chamber, two hundred, two hundred and fifty, all the way up to three hundred and twenty-six, and by then she was gasping, her heart pounding and she was in the upper chamber, and he was there, all white with his two ginger splotches, shivering, whiskers quivering, velvet ears flat against his back, looking so worried, thinking he'd been abandoned, and she swept him up in her arms and wondered how anyone could be so cruel.

There was a door that led outside to the parapet that encircled the tip of the tower. The day blazed clear and bright, every trace of fog now gone. Clutching His Nibs, Caro stepped outside and looked down.

One hundred and sixty-three feet below, a figure hurried away towards Belvedere Road, a figure in a headscarf and a drab raincoat, pushing a pram.

Emerald Standing.

Heading for the Rubbles.

She looked like she was almost *skipping*.

Caro fled back down the staircase, taking care not to lose her footing now that she was clutching her darling rabbit, but when she reached the bottom of the steps, no chink of light came through the heavy door.

It was very, very firmly shut.

She didn't want to ever let go of His Nibs now that she had got him back, but still, she set him down and began to search for something that she could use to open the door with. But she couldn't find a handle, or a bolt, or a key or a lever ... in fact there didn't seem to be any mechanism for opening the door at all.

She kicked at it, hard, and knocked and pummelled, and shouted 'Help!!!' and 'Let us out!' but it was no good; her voice sounded small and frail, lost inside the thick brick walls. His Nibs gave a helpful squeak. But no one was there to hear.

Back up the stairs again, round and round, His Nibs heavy now, his little eyes gleaming, wondering what was going on. Past the first gallery, up to the second one. Back outside onto the parapet surrounded by an iron balustrade.

Caro peered over the railing. But sure enough, just as there was no way to climb up, there was no way to climb down either. Sheer, forbidding brick wall. Not a single foothold.

On the river, a pleasure boat steamed by; it was crammed with sightseers and Caro shouted and waved frantically but nobody looked up. They were all facing the other way, waiting for a glimpse of the Houses of Parliament.

'What are we going to do?' she asked His Nibs. 'She's going to get away with it. She's going to get the real painting from the car. And somehow she'll pin the blame on Ronnie or Jacinta. We can't let that happen!'

They *had* to catch up with Emerald. Prove that *she* was the criminal.

Caro and His Nibs descended the spiral staircase again. This time she counted the windows. One, two, three, four, five in total. She stopped at the bottom one and opened it, the hinges squeaking in protest. She stuck her head out hopefully, but hope drained away as she saw she was about forty feet above the ground. The opening was narrow, but not too narrow to squeeze through, so she clambered out onto the ledge to have a proper look. It was miles too far to jump, unless you wanted to break both ankles. She couldn't jump with His Nibs anyway.

She retreated back inside, feeling useless, not being able to do anything. She wondered if Toby was still locked in his room. If he wasn't, would he have telephoned Ronnie by now? Please, yes, she thought.

She peered out of the window again. Oh! There were trees, young ones, planted a short way away from the tower. Could she make a jump for the nearest one? The tops of the branches swayed in the breeze. They looked ever so fragile. They might not carry her weight but it was worth risking it.

Before she could change her mind, she picked up His Nibs, and draped him, like a thick scarf, around her neck and shoulders. He wasn't too happy about it and shifted uncomfortably but he stayed put. His warmth and his pattering heart were comforting. Very carefully, Caro clambered out of the window again, so that she was crouching on the narrow ledge. If she missed ...

she wouldn't miss! She couldn't miss! It didn't bear thinking about. But before she could try, the rabbit hopped off her shoulders and bounded back through the window and into the safety of the tower.

'Hey,' she called. 'We can do it!' And she followed him back inside and scooped him up and draped him over her shoulders again.

But as soon as she was crouched back on the outside ledge, poised to leap, the rabbit sprang off her shoulders again and escaped back inside the tower.

'Don't you trust me?' she asked him, following him inside. He looked back at her, blinking. Twitched his nose. *No.*

He didn't. And she couldn't force him to.

Caro sat down on the spiral staircase; buried her head in her hands. Everything felt hopeless. Emerald would be long gone soon. She would somehow stick the whole thing on Ronnie. The pub would be closed and—

'Caro!' From outside the narrow window came a shout.

Caro sprang up.

Joy leapt into her chest.

It was Horace.

And he was shouting something through his cupped hands. 'Look in Albie's rucksack Caro!'

The rucksack? Still on her back. Something sharp sticking into her spine.

She pulled it off and unbuckled it. Stared inside.

A mess of wool and knitting needles.

The escape she'd been looking for.

Albie's knitting-needle ladder!

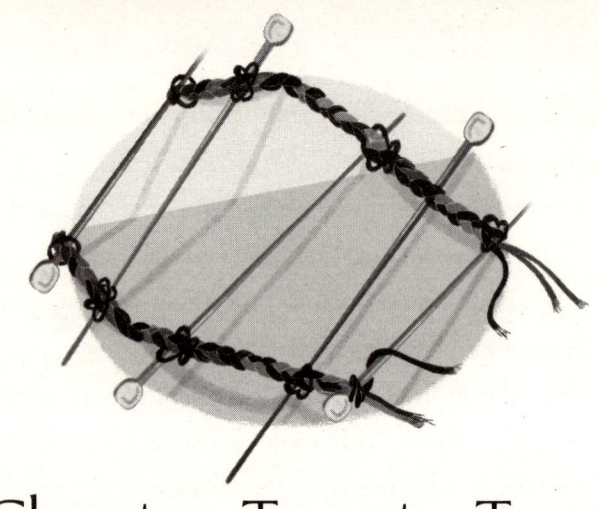

Chapter Twenty-Two

The knitting-needle ladder click-clacked as Caro unfurled it. It seemed like it had grown. Twenty rungs made with size-thirteen knitting needles; the wool doubled up and plaited into thick strong rope to link the rungs together.

'Albie's been busy,' she cried to His Nibs, and she was laughing out loud because she couldn't believe that she had such ingenious friends. How had Albie known? And Horace – he must have run like the wind to get here. She felt like she was overflowing with gratitude.

She tied the ladder to some railings surrounding a hole where, once upon a time, slabs of lead would have been hoisted up. She draped His Nibs round her shoulders again, and this time he stayed put.

Then she climbed down.

'The police are on their way,' said Horace when she reached the bottom. He could barely contain his excitement. 'The Bully Boys came up trumps. Shut Rob and Ray in the gallery while I ran to alert the authorities. But ...' He looked round. Looked back at Caro. Realised something was wrong.

'What happened? Where is she?'

'Gone,' said Caro. 'Took *The Nightingale* and went to get *The Thrush*.'

'No! The real one?'

Caro nodded. 'In the Rubbles.'

* * *

They could hear the police sirens as they approached the Rubbles. They agreed that Horace would wait on Belvedere Road to flag them down.

As soon as Caro entered the patch of wasteland, she could see someone emerging from the old beaten-up car. Someone dressed in a drab raincoat, with a headscarf knotted tightly under her chin. Someone wearing round tinted glasses.

Clutching His Nibs close to her chest, Caro took a deep breath.

'*Cou-rage*,' she said to herself, just like Victor had said to her two weeks ago. Then she walked fast, striding towards the woman, her heart pounding; adrenalin rising. The woman hadn't seen her yet. She was tucking the painting into the pram.

Caro kept her footsteps light.

'Mrs Standing!' she called when she was quite close, just a few feet away.

The woman stopped. She turned. Even behind the tinted glasses Caro could see her eyes were murderous. Burning black coals, crackling and spitting.

'You?' she said, her voice low and venomous. 'How did you get out from that tower?'

Caro needed to keep Emerald here somehow, just until the police arrived. Horace had said they were on their way. She took a step forward.

'Get away from me,' spat Emerald Starling. 'If you and Bunny know what's good for you.'

Caro couldn't hear the sirens any more. Please don't let that mean they'd gone the wrong way. Had they not seen Horace? She took another step towards Emerald. His Nibs quivered a warning in her arms. *Be careful, Caro.*

'Stay right where you are,' said Emerald, her words knife-sharp, her right hand reaching inside her left cuff, and drawing something out that was small and glittering. She pointed it at Caro as if she was about to throw a dart. It wasn't a dart, though. It was a blade, smaller than the one Rob had flashed in the kitchen, but just as lethal. The tip winked in the last of the late afternoon sun.

'Come any closer,' whispered Emerald, 'and I'll pierce the heart of that fluffy monstrosity you're carrying.'

His Nibs seemed to shrink in Caro's arms and his ears went flat.

'Now be a dear and get out of my way.' Emerald flicked the knife menacingly and the snake tattoo on her wrist revealed itself for an instant before slipping back inside her cuff. 'I really should have finished that thing off yesterday.'

'No!' shouted Caro, and then everything happened very quickly. Emerald Standing drew back her arm, took aim and threw the knife straight at her. At the same time, a black-clad figure leapt out from behind the car, grabbed His Nibs out of Caro's arms and shoved Caro out of harm's way.

It was such a violent shove that Caro stumbled to her knees.

The knife clattered to the floor.

'Don't you touch her!'

Caro looked up, confused. What had just happened? Where was His Nibs? Who had just spoken? And why was she on the ground?

Then she saw.

Gam!

Gam, holding the rabbit and planting her frail body squarely between Caro and Emerald.

Except all of a sudden she didn't *seem* frail, thought Caro. She looked strong.

For a moment, Emerald seemed to freeze. And then she looked beyond Gam and Caro, and let out a long, low hiss.

'Caro! I've been looking for you everywhere. I telephoned...'

It was Toby, staring at them in bewilderment. Caro watched him take in the scene. Clock Emerald Standing – who was just that second reaching for the knife.

In an instant he shot forward and snatched it up before she could. 'Stay there!' he shouted, pointing it at her, 'or I'll...'

'You haven't got the bottle,' spat Emerald, but she was backing away, dragging the pram with her, bump, bump across the Rubbles and...

A crash of twigs, a spray of bamboo sticks, a splatter of mud and weeds, an almighty smash and ...

Emerald Standing disappeared.

'What?' yelped Toby.

The trap! Caro could barely believe it. She scrambled up and let out a whoop. Emerald Standing had fallen into the very same hole that Tom had!

And she'd never be able to get out. She wasn't a gymnast like Tom.

A chorus of approaching voices, from the other side of the Rubbles: Horace, the Bully Boys, and then the roar of an engine, and a police car smashed right through the gates that were always locked and screeched to a halt by the tyre swings.

Caro flung herself at Horace. Hugged him tight.

'Thank you, thank you!' she said.

And this time, he hugged her back as though he would never let go, and he said, 'We did it, Caro, we did it.'

'We got 'em. Rob and Ray!' shouted Stanley.

'We turned 'em in!' yelled Carl.

And Caro shouted back, 'And we got her!'

'Caro.' A quiet voice. Not remotely sharp. A bit hesitant.

It was Gam holding out His Nibs, and when Caro

had taken him from her, she stooped down to pluck up her trusty green silk umbrella, which she'd had to abandon temporarily when she had shoved Caro to safety.

'How did you know I was here?' Caro asked.

Gam, in the *Rubbles*. It was extraordinary.

'Tom told me of course,' said Gam. 'Said this is your favourite place.'

'You saved His Nibs ... but I thought ...' It didn't make sense!

'I made a mistake about the rabbit,' Gam said bluntly. 'I should have said something yesterday ... but ... anyway, I came to tell you ... And then when I saw that woman' – she looked disbelievingly towards the hole which the police had now surrounded – 'about to attack, I was damned if I was going to let anything happen to him. Or you.'

'Thank you,' said Caro softly. Gam had rescued her. If she hadn't turned up at that moment ... It was too awful to think about.

'Caro,' said Gam, and then she drew a great breath and spoke very rapidly. 'I didn't mean to push you away. It wasn't fair to blame you for ... everything I've done wrong.'

Caro leaned over the side of the pram. Pulled back

the covers. There they were, three paintings, all nestled together. *The Thrush*, *The Skylark* and *The Nightingale*.

'I know,' Caro said truthfully. 'But let's not worry about that now.'

Chapter Twenty-Three

On the other side of the river, quite faint but still within hearing distance, Big Ben struck five.

It had been a long day.

It seemed aeons ago that Caro had woken to the suffocating London fog, confused, scared and unaware that even worse things lay ahead. Now, dusk was falling and the cobbled back streets of Waterloo were suffused with a pinky-orange glow.

The police – six constables, two sergeants and an inspector – had been and gone, taking with them all three paintings and a furious Emerald Standing. The Bully Boys had been called in for their teas; now Horace, Toby, Gam and Caro made their way back to the pub.

'Tell me again, why you came?' asked Caro. She still couldn't quite believe that it was Gam who had saved His Nibs. Gam who had been so strict, who had such a terrible aversion to rabbits, who seemed to be opposed to freedom of all sorts.

'I came to make amends,' said Gam, and then she stopped.

She was looking beyond Caro, further down the street.

Caro turned to follow her gaze.

There, outside the pub, was Albie. And next to him, a tall, bulky-looking fellow: a gentleman wearing several coats, with a long browny-red beard and a sack on a stick slung over one shoulder.

Albie had brought Victor, just like she had asked him to.

And even though she'd intended to quiz Victor first, see if everything she had thought was true, now she saw that wouldn't be necessary.

As it turned out, all she had to do was watch.

Time stretched.

No one said anything. They just knew not to.

And then ...

'Victor!' Gam whispered. And then louder, 'Victor!'

And Caro had a most peculiar feeling. A moment

of release ... like the feeling you get after you've been holding your breath for ages. A swish, a swoop.

A sweet moment.

Then Victor began to move, and Gam almost ran towards him.

'It *was* you! I knew I saw you ... on the heath ... when I was out walking last week ...' Gam stumbled a little, as if felled by the enormity of the situation and Caro moved closer and put a steadying hand on her arm.

'I've been waiting and waiting for you to come back.' Her voice trembled as she spoke.

'I didn't know if you wanted me to, Mary,' said Victor carefully. The way he spoke was as if every word mattered. As if the slightest mistake could not be made. Caro had never seen a face so full of concern.

'I'm sorry, I'm sorry!' Gam cried. 'I was rotten, I am rotten, I would understand if you never wanted to come back.'

'Mary! I'm the one who should be sorry,' said Victor quickly. And he dropped his sack with a thud and stepped towards Gam, his arms wide.

Behind them, the door to the pub opened and a small, tough-looking woman in a flowery apron emerged. She was holding a dustpan and brush and she emptied it briskly, watching as the dust billowed into the air. When the task was done, she tapped the dustpan once, twice on the kerb. Only then did she look up and take in the scene in front of her.

Her mouth dropped open.

'Caro Monday! What in God's name is going on? And where on earth have *you* been Toby-me-lad?'

'Ronnie!' said Caro, and the relief that swept over her was so intense it was almost unbearable. 'You're back!'

She shoved His Nibs into Horace's arms and launched herself at her other mother. She breathed in the smell of cinnamon and nutmeg and felt the soft cotton of the flower-sprigged apron against her cheek. Ronnie's hug was warm and strong and full of vigour. But after some moments, Ronnie gently released her. The publican had questions. And she needed answers.

'Toby rang to say I needed to come home urgently. And, well, now I can see why. The place is a tip! My best vase is broken! The glasses don't look like they've been washed in days, there's rubbish all over the place and ... Luckily it coincided with Harry's return, so I could leave Marjorie. Where *is* that Mrs Standing? I'm going to give her a piece of my mind.'

'You're not going to like it,' said Caro. 'When you hear what's been going on—'

'Mrs Rudd?'

It was Gam, standing extremely close to Victor.

'Who's enquiring?' asked Ronnie. Her eyes swept over the small crowd hovering expectantly outside her pub. Horace and Toby she knew, of course, but who was the skinny little boy? Who was this man with the beard and the pack who looked very much like a gentleman of the road? And who was this elderly lady in the severe black dress, clutching a green silk umbrella as if her life depended on it even though there was no promise of rain?

'Ronnie...' started Caro. But there was so much to explain. 'It's all right, Caro,' said Gam. 'Mrs Rudd, I'm Mary Monday, Jacinta's aunt.'

Caro noticed that instead of rapping her umbrella on the ground to match her words, she was passing it from hand to hand, almost as if she was nervous.

'Oh!' said Ronnie, and her face cleared but she didn't look happy. 'Well, thank you for agreeing to look after Caro at such short notice. I wouldn't have asked if it wasn't important.'

'Is Jacinta here?' asked Gam tentatively.

'She's on her way back. Only went and got herself caught up in that Panamanian coup with her pal Margot Fonteyn.'

'She's all right?!' said Caro. 'So it *was* just a scrape!'

'A scrape to end all scrapes,' said Ronnie. 'But...' She looked at Gam. 'If you don't mind me saying so, she won't be too happy to find you here when she arrives. Even though you did help me out when I was in a fix.'

Caro watched as Gam seemed to shrink a little, take a step back, and bow her head.

'Of course,' she said, 'you are quite right. It's getting late and... Albie, come on, time to make tracks...'

Caro stared.

'No!' she blurted. 'Don't go!'

Gam lifted her head. Glanced from Caro to Ronnie, to Victor.

It couldn't end like this.

'Caro,' said Ronnie. 'There's tons to do. Your great-aunt has been very accommodating I'm sure but—'

'Ronnie!' burst out Caro. 'Please...'

Everyone was looking at her. Horace's eyes were saying 'go on, Caro'; Albie was nodding encouragingly.

'... you've always said there were two sides to every story, *and* you said family was important,' said Caro.

And with utter clarity she realised that it was imperative they listen to Gam's story right now. All of a sudden she had to know *everything*.

Why had Victor gone tramping all over the country for years and years and only just come home?

What had Gam done?

And why hadn't Jacinta forgiven her?

'Maybe ...' said Victor as if he could read Caro's mind. 'If it's all right with you, Mrs Rudd, might we all come in and have a cup of tea? I think a few explanations might be in order.'

'Well ...' said Ronnie. She didn't look convinced.

'Please!' begged Caro.

'Please, Mrs Rudd,' echoed Horace.

'Please, please,' said Albie.

They were good friends, thought Caro.

'Sounds like a good idea, Mrs Rudd,' added Toby.

'Look who's talking,' said Ronnie. 'Well, all right, but you'd better be quick. Jacinta'll be home any minute. And on top of that, I've got a million things to do to get this pub in order before we can open the doors again.'

* * *

Despite Jacinta's imminent arrival, Ronnie was adamant that nothing could be explained until the pub was shipshape.

Toby swept up and washed the floor and put things away.

Horace polished the glasses until they sparkled.

Caro and Albie helped Ronnie make cups of tea.

Marks and Tom turned up out of the blue, arm in arm, with a packet of biscuits.

His Nibs lolloped about happily, pleased to have the run of the saloon once more.

Victor and Gam didn't do anything. They just sat in the velvet chairs, so close to each other that their knees touched. Albie nudged Caro.

'They're holding hands,' he whispered.

When everything was in order, they all sat down and Caro started by relating the events of the past few days. Horace and Albie did the actions.

Ronnie nearly fell off her stool when Caro got to the bit about the confrontation in the cellar. 'Toby, I've a mind to sack you here and now for bringing those hoodlums into my pub.'

'I wouldn't blame you if you did, Mrs Rudd,' he said, hanging his head.

'But you can't, Ronnie,' said Caro. 'If he hadn't arrived in the Rubbles when he did ...'

It was quite amazing, thought Caro, how it had been Toby and Gam, of all people, who had saved her and His Nibs's lives.

'I'll think about it,' said Ronnie as she turned her

attention back to Gam and Victor. 'Jacinta will be here soon and goodness knows what she'll say when she sees this welcome committee. But you wanted to explain... and it seems young Caro is bursting to hear what you've got to say, so...'

Gam swallowed. She glanced at Victor who gave her an encouraging smile.

Horace moved over to Caro and quietly took her hand. Albie, who had been playing with His Nibbs, hopped up and took the other one.

'We were always a happy family,' Gam began. 'Me, Victor, Billy (our son, who would've been your uncle, Caro) and Jacinta, who came to live with us when she was not much more than two years old. Her parents, Victor's sister and her husband, had died suddenly and unexpectedly and there was never any question that we wouldn't care for our niece, whom we adored.

'It was during the war that everything changed.' Gam's eyes had gone all watery. Victor patted her hand. 'When the children were evacuated.'

'Sent away?' asked Caro. She knew all about the wartime evacuees. They'd learned about them at school. Sent out of town to stay with other families – complete strangers – to keep them safe during the Blitz.

'Mmm,' said Gam.

She reached out to His Nibs, who was busily working his way through a carrot top, and prodded one of his velvety ears. 'Billy was only nine. He loved his rabbit. He was called Ginger. You remember Ginger, don't you?' she asked Tom.

'Wait,' said Caro to Tom. 'I thought you said Great Aunt Mary didn't remember you? That you missed the moment when you could tell her that you were once Billy's friend?'

'We talked it over,' said Tom. 'Got it all out in the open this morning, before Mary came to find you, Caro.'

'Shall I carry on?' said Gam, a touch of her old imperiousness reappearing. Caro and Albie exchanged glances and she knew they were both thinking the same thing. It was actually quite a relief to see a hint of the old Gam.

'Billy pleaded and pleaded to take Ginger with him, but I said no. It wouldn't be possible.'

Caro caught Ronnie's eye. It was just like her not wanting Caro to take His Nibs to Hampstead. She didn't hold it against Ronnie though. She'd been doing her best, just as, presumably, Gam had been doing hers.

'Billy and Jacinta were sent to stay with a family in Kent, and from the start they weren't happy,' continued

Gam. 'They were terribly homesick and they wrote letters begging to come home. They said Mrs King – I think that was her name – wasn't kind. And ...'

Gam let out a big shuddery sigh. 'The thing is, they *could've* come home at that point!' She looked anguished. 'Early on in the war, there wasn't any bombing. Everyone was waiting for it to start, but it didn't come. People called it the phony war and some of them fetched their children back. Not me. Several times I nearly got on the train to go and get them, but then I always decided against it. In the end I thought it was better to be safe than sorry. After all, they did have each other. They were very close.'

Caro pictured a young Jacinta and Billy in the countryside. She thought how much she had missed the pub when she first went to Hampstead – so much it had almost hurt – and how when Gam had wanted to separate her from His Nibs she had actually thought she would die.

'And then the bombs did come,' Gam said. 'Night after night. And I was *glad* they were safe in the country. I didn't know that things were so bad they were planning to run away.'

'Were they really?' asked Albie.

Gam nodded. 'Afterwards, Jacinta tried to tell me

it was a mixture of Mrs King, homesickness and Billy missing Ginger. She said their plan was simply to come and see the rabbit, but beyond that, they hadn't really thought it through.'

Gam sighed again.

'How were *they* to know that I'd already sent Ginger to stay with a friend in the suburbs? I'd driven out the week before and left him there. So ... Billy didn't even get to hold Ginger before ...' Her words faded away to nothing.

'It's all right Mary, it's all right,' said Victor gently.

'The bomb fell on a house in the next street. The blast ricocheting through the back gardens. Debris blew out all over the place. Billy was hit by a piece of flying concrete, or a lump of iron – I don't know – whatever it is that holds houses together until they explode.'

The air in the room seemed to change. Caro's eyes felt hot. Horace, registering the enormity of the situation, squeezed her hand.

It sounded terrible. Unbearable. Caro tried to picture it, but it was too awful and she shoved the image away. All fire and brimstone, like hell, if there was a hell. She understood now why Jacinta didn't like to talk about the war.

'I didn't even *try* to listen to Jacinta's explanations,'

continued Gam. 'I blamed her for bringing Billy home. She was a year older you see. I sent her straight back to Kent. I couldn't even speak to her. The same with Victor. When he came home ... I felt like I was in a black dark hole.'

'You sent Mum back to Mrs King's?' asked Caro in disbelief. 'After *that*?'

'It was a mistake,' Gam mumbled. 'I can see that now. The worst mistake I ever made.'

'What a mess,' said Ronnie. Even so, there was sympathy in her gaze.

'Jacinta stayed in Kent for the rest of the war. Four years. When she came home, she was fourteen. Of course she couldn't forgive me for how I behaved towards her. And the truth was, I couldn't bear to see her without Billy.'

'And then what happened? Was Victor still at home, then?' asked Albie.

'Not much, no,' admitted Victor. 'I was away for work a lot and when I was at home ...'

'It wasn't a happy place,' said Gam. 'By then I was terrified something would happen to Jacinta. I wouldn't let her out of my sight, or go out, or do any of the things normal fourteen-year-olds should do. We rowed a lot. She said living with me was worse than being in Kent with Mrs King. That it was like being in prison.'

'It didn't help that I was away so much,' said Victor.

'Everything fell apart. I drove them away. First of all, Jacinta – as soon as she turned sixteen, she was off. And then Victor. He tried – you did, Victor, you know you did – but I shut you out. And look!' she turned to Albie and Caro. 'Here I am, doing the same to you.'

Victor cleared his throat. 'It's not all your fault, Mary. We both had a hand in breaking up our family. I went on the road because I couldn't face up to our difficulties. It was the easy way out. To escape.'

All that sadness, thought Caro, trying to make sense of it. And all those wasted years. What would it be like if someone she loved died? Horace. Or Ronnie. Or Mum. Would it make her act like Gam had?

She thought she understood – a tiny bit – why Gam had behaved in such a peculiar way towards her and Albie. She had been protecting herself. She hadn't wanted to get too close to them in case they left her too.

And Caro *had* left. In that respect she had proved Gam right.

Caro picked up His Nibs and rubbed her forehead against his. Then she crossed over to Gam and said, 'Can I?'

And Gam looked at the rabbit and up at Caro, and said, 'Yes.'

Very gently, Caro lowered His Nibs down onto Gam's lap and showed her how to gently stroke the rabbit's velvety ears. There were still a lot of tangles in Jacinta and Gam's and Victor's stories to unravel. But getting Gam to accept the rabbit was a start.

Once upon a time the Mondays had been a happy family.

Caro remembered Tom saying how he had dreamed of being part of a family like that. What a shame to let it all go. Surely Billy wouldn't have wanted that?

'Can't you start again?' she asked Gam.

She saw a glimmer of hope light up Gam's eyes.

'If you'll let me,' she said. 'And you, Albie. I haven't done a very good job with you so far, have I?'

Albie shrugged. 'It's all right, Mrs Monday. You tried your best.'

Caro looked at Albie, and her heart seemed to melt a little. Albie, dear Albie. He sounded so old and wise. Albie who had lost his parents so young. Who had suffered such loss. Out of all of them, he was probably the one who understood Gam the most.

'But I'd like your parents to be proud of me,' said Gam. 'I know they'd be proud of you.'

'Do you think so?' said Albie in a very small voice.
'I do,' said Gam.

'What do *you* say, sonny-boy?' Caro whispered to her dear darling rabbit. 'Do you think everything is going to be all right?'

He snuffled and blinked at her sweetly, '*Yes.*'

'I think so too,' said Caro.

'Another cup of tea, anyone?' said Ronnie, standing up and starting to collect the crockery.

'Listen!' said Albie.

Far away was the sound of someone whistling.

On Gam's lap, His Nibs pricked up his ears.

'Caro!' said Horace, his face lighting up. 'Is that your…'

The whistling grew louder, the tune became more beautiful, the notes so full of sweetness and yearning, dipping and soaring, that it was impossible not to fall under its spell. It was the same tune Caro had thought she'd heard on Hampstead Heath with Horace that day. 'The Flower Duet'. The tune that Jacinta always whistled when she was on her way home.

Now Victor started to whistle it too.

'Two sides to every story remember, Gam?' said Caro, jumping up and hugging first Horace, then Albie, then Ronnie. 'Thank you,' she said to each of them in turn.

Gam smiled, a small, brave smile. 'Yes, Caro. I shall listen this time.'

And Caro ran to open the door.

LONDON DAILY NEWS

Today, the acclaimed ballerina Margot Fonteyn, best known for her duets with Rudolf Nureyev, arrived back in Great Britain, shortly after the British Ambassador secured her release from Panama. In a bizarre series of events, Fonteyn was accused of plotting a military coup with her husband, the diplomat Robert Arias. The Foreign Office Minister John Profumo described the whole episode as 'a slap-dash comedy'. 'Dame Margot,' said Profumo, 'was at pains to say that her husband's intentions were strictly honourable and that, although he realised that revolutions were not very pleasant things, he was prepared to go to any extremes to help the ordinary people of Panama who ... were having a raw deal.' A number of the ballerina's friends, holidaying with her at the time – including the celebrated whistler Jacinta Monday – became inadvertently caught up in events. Thankfully, all are now safe and well and back at home.

Epilogue

Six years later

APRIL 1965

The girl got up at the crack of dawn because she wanted to get over to Hampstead Heath early.

Moving quietly so as not to wake anyone, she washed and dressed, and fetched the old picnic basket up from the cellar. In the kitchen, she boiled some eggs, cut bread for sandwiches, wrapped a fruit cake in wax paper, and filled flasks with hot water for tea.

Once she was ready, it was a quick dash through

the still silent streets of Waterloo to the London Underground. Her journey wasn't a long one, only eleven stops on the tube, and soon she was striding across the heath.

The girl stretched and did a happy little skip. She felt good. The sky was blue; the grass tips had turned a sort of greeny-gold in the sun. It was going to be a lovely day.

At last she came to the place she was looking for. The place they called the Wilds.

Not much had changed. It was still all untamed, with grass growing tall like prairie grass, odd stumpy trees and thickety bushes running rampant. The girl came here often: in late spring when it was a riot of daisies and buttercups; in summer when it straggled with sweet-smelling dog roses; in autumn when there were blackberries to pick.

The balancing beam was there of course, souped up with the many additions that the girl's mother had built over the years. Now it was more of an adventure playground – with ladders and turrets, and tunnels and hidey holes – a favourite with the local children: a happy place echoing with joyous cries all year round.

The girl lay in the long grass and pointed her toes. Next week she would be off on a tour with the acrobatic troupe that she was part of. Just the thought of it filled her with joy. Of course it would mean saying goodbye to her best of best friends. But he was off on an adventure all of his own, to Paris, to take up a place at the Institut de la Mode. It was a dream come true. The first step in his journey to becoming a fashion designer.

Towards noon, the guests began to arrive. First, the girl's two mothers, one a tiny bird of a woman, the other taller, more flamboyant, with a shock of long chestnut-coloured hair; then her best friend, so stylish he looked as though he had stepped out of the pages of a fashion magazine. A little later, an earnest-looking boy of about fourteen turned up with an elderly couple – the girl's great-aunt and great-uncle. Lastly, came a family: a young man with an abundance of bright red hair; a young woman in paint-splattered overalls, and a gaggle of small children.

The girl listened happily to the chatter and the laughter. Later, her mother – the whistling one – entertained them all with her repertoire. It was wonderful, stretching all the way from the Beatles to Ella Fitzgerald to *Madame Butterfly*. When she had finished, there was much clapping and whooping, the other mother's voice loudest and proudest of all.

After the picnic was demolished, the young family went on a mission for ice cream and fizzy drinks and chips. It was a good day. The sort where the adults say, 'Yes, go on then, why not,' instead of the usual 'No'.

As the sun began to sink, the girl wandered off to a small cherry tree. She'd planted it with her great-uncle three years ago to this very day. The blossom fluttered in the breeze prettily, like pink-white snow.

The girl slid down so that she was sitting with her back against the tree trunk. Very carefully, as if she was unpacking a set of the finest bone china, she allowed herself to remember the two ginger patches, the ears, soft as velvet, the pitter-patter of his heart.

Thank you, she said in her head. For all that extra love you gave me when Mum was away.

'You all right?' It was her mother and behind her, her great-aunt.

'Just remembering,' she said.

'Let's remember together,' said her mother, and she sat down beside her. Together they stretched out their arms to the elderly woman and she sat down too, even though her knees were a bit creaky.

The cherry tree was where they came to remember the girl's rabbit, and the great-aunt's son, who'd also been the girl's mother's cousin.

They were a complicated family. Sometimes, families just are.

'You're one in a million, you know that, right?' said the girl's mother.

'*You* are,' said the girl.

'And you,' said the girl's mother to the great-aunt.

The girl felt a glow of pride. Once upon a time, her mother and great-aunt's relationship had been very, very tangled. But over the years they had managed to smooth things out.

Now the great-uncle strolled over.

'Hear that?' he said.

They all listened. Somewhere nearby a bird was in full song.

A thrush? Or a nightingale? Or maybe even a skylark?

The girl grinned because, after all, it was a songbird who had brought them all together.

In a roundabout sort of way.

Acknowledgements

This is very much a London story, so I would like to thank my parents for opening my eyes to this wonderful, wild, beautiful city: the trips to the theatre, the excursions to the ballet, the outings to the big museums on rainy weekends, the journeys on the Jubilee and Northern lines; the drives along the Finchley Road, turning left at Swiss Cottage, past the big old houses on Adelaide Road (where you could see straight into the front rooms as they were being demolished) down to Camden Town and up to the West End.

Although I would never have dreamed of climbing it as Caro does, memories of the old Hungerford Bridge

– the thundering trains, the narrow walkway, the glimpses of the swirling black water below – are still vivid. It was a place both wonderful and terrible at the same time, and it was this image that made me want to write Caro's story.

Onto these memories are layered fictional and pictorial representations of London. A jumble of Charles Dickens, Noel Streatfeild, and photographic collections of children at play: in the street, on bombsites, in ramshackle adventure playgrounds. The Play Well exhibition at the Wellcome Collection was really helpful, as were the photographs of Roger Mayne, who captured London street life in the 1950's so eloquently.

Real life is always stranger than fiction, and the story about Margot Fonteyn being involved in an attempted Panamanian coup is true. Also, a knitting needle ladder was famously used by the spy George Blake to escape Wormwood Scrubs prison in 1966. The ladder consisted of 20 rungs of size 13 grey plastic knitting needles. Blake's escape was widely reported at the time, but the extent of Fonteyn's role in the coup didn't come to light until 2010, when confidential government files were released to the National Archives and which I read about in *The Guardian*.

My thanks to the team at Faber for helping me bring this book to life. Thank you to Alice for being such a brilliant and inspiring editor. Thank you also to Natasha Brown, Bethany Carter, Ama Badu, Emma Eldridge, Leah Thaxton, Sarah Connell and Simi Toor for taking the best care of me and my books. Thank you to Maurice Lyon for your spot on copy editing (and for pointing out that you can't actually see the golden dome of the Monument from Hungerford Bridge!). To Kim Geyer for your inspired illustrations, they are, as always, beautiful. And to my agent Lucy Irvine, for looking after me so well.

Thank you to my first readers: Heather, Margot, Nick, and my mum Moira – I really appreciate your time and your comments.

Thank you to all the booksellers, librarians, bloggers and reviewers, your support is invaluable. And last but very much not least, thank you reader, for choosing this book.

SHORTLISTED
Edward Stanford Children's Travel Book of the Year Award

Judith Eagle
THE ACCIDENTAL STOWAWAY

'Pacy, witty, I absolutely adored it.'
EMMA CARROLL

ILLUSTRATED BY KIM GEYER

Liverpool, 1910
Patch finds adventure on every deck of the 'floating palace' she accidentally stows away on.

'FABULOUS!'
Emma Carroll, author of *Letters from the Lighthouse*

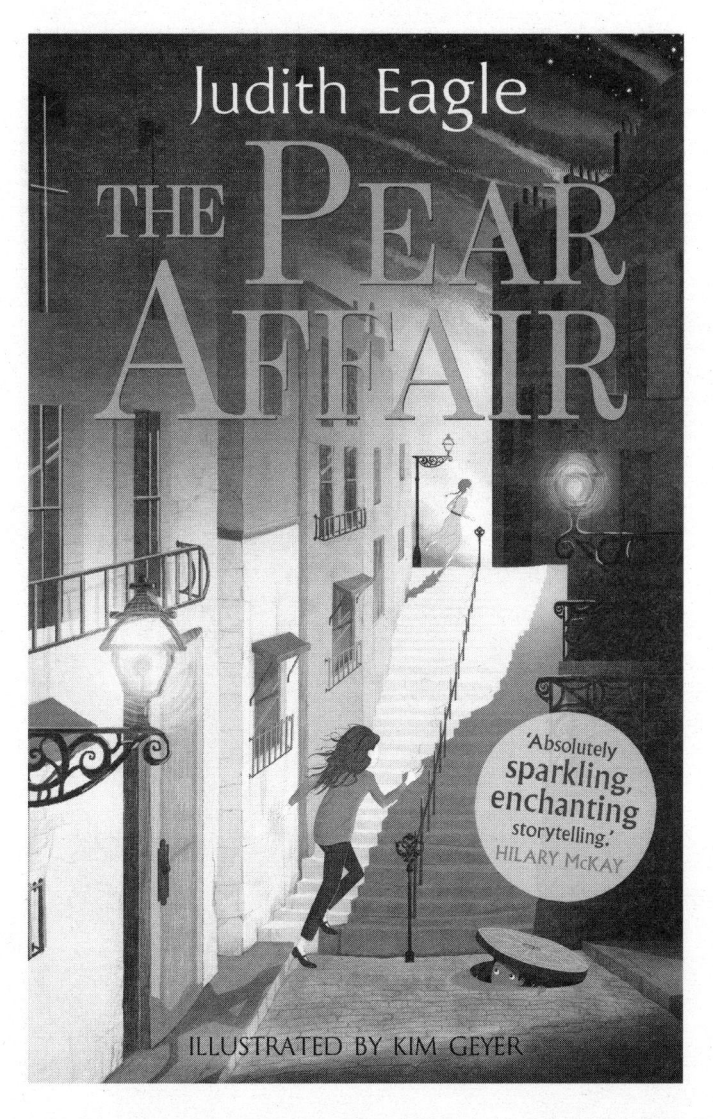

Judith Eagle
THE PEAR AFFAIR

'Absolutely **sparkling, enchanting** storytelling.'
HILARY McKAY

ILLUSTRATED BY KIM GEYER

A spectacular adventure set through and under the streets of Paris. Nell must solve an extraordinary mystery in order to be reunited with her beloved Pear.

'A riveting adventure.'
The Guardian

Judith Eagle
THE SECRET STARLING

'An absolute joy of a read.'
EMMA CARROLL

ILLUSTRATED BY KIM GEYER

Abandoned children running wild on the moors, evil child catchers, cunning cats and mysterious ballet shoes abound in this incredible novel.